RETIRED: Now What?

FRED LICHTENBERG

Printed in the United States on permanent paper

First Edition

ISBN-13: 978-1505342925

First Printing December 2014

Edited by: Susan Bryant at Editorguru.com

Kindle Edition by Ted Risk at dellasterdesign.com

www.fredlichtenberg.com

For the Baby Boomers

ACKNOWLEDGMENTS

Parts of the book were researched through interviews and online information, and I owe those people and the WWW a big thanks. Thanks also to a dear friend, Joe Enrico, who read the draft and offered terrific suggestions. To my wife, Sonia, my first line of defense for the written word, and who keeps me out of literary trouble.

PROLOGUE

THE END OF A LENGTHY SENTENCE

"Are you still here?"

My head shot up from my desk. I looked around but didn't see a soul—for the second time today. Either I was hearing things—indicating my decision to retire was perfect timing—or someone was playing games. I stood, looked around. Must be me.

I called my wife, Kate, but got her voice mail. Nice. I sat down and sighed. Had I really made the right decision to retire? It's too late anyway. My papers were in and probably processed. HR had sent over some pimple-faced kid around three o'clock to finalize my government service. He was polite even while shoving clearance forms under my nose. With every signature, I turned over pieces of my career: my credentials with a photograph that looked younger than my son and a building pass with a photo from before I started using Just for Men products. With trepidation, I turned in my laptop, praying I hadn't left any incriminating personal stuff on my hard drive.

The kid looked too serious, but he had a tough job checking off the received column, stopping occasionally to review the form. He asked for the keys to my file cabinet and desk, which, the desk, like me, was broken and rendered useless years ago. I kept that secret from Mister Serious.

He stuck his head in my personnel folder, drumming his fingers on the desk while viewing the top-secret documents, putting me in a trance until I asked, "You have anything else for me to sign? I gotta get back to work."

He closed the file. "I guess that's it, Mr. Short."

I watched the kid load up a cart and wheel off with my career. "Hey, you got a name?"

He stopped. "Me? It's Julian."

"Well, Julian, I hope you're as happy here as I've been."

"Hope so, Mr. Short. I like it here."

"Yeah, me too, but it's time for me to go."

Julian nodded indifferently.

"You're too young to understand that right now."

He nodded again. "Guess so, Mr. Short."

"It's Eddie, by the way."

He nodded. "Eddie."

I watched Julian disappear through the door until my OCD took over and I checked my file cabinet and desk for the umpteenth time.

Regardless of the paperwork I signed off on, it still was too late to stick around. Fifty coworkers had thrown a luncheon in my honor today at a local country club and showered me with gifts. And I wasn't about to give up those gift cards; I needed a new watch.

Where was Kate? I speed-dialed her number again, left another message. God, I needed a sympathetic ear. Wait a minute! I should be calling my son, Jesse, instead. He's the therapist in the family. Another speed-dial, another message. He must be with a patient. Great. Now what?

I leaned back in my chair and closed my eyes, feeling vulnerable, still questioning if I had made the right decision. And like a vision, my mother appeared. I smiled. She always managed to ease my anxieties in times of uncertainty. I couldn't call her, of course; she passed away years ago. I searched back to my New York days growing up in a chaotic household. Drunken father, soothing mother. What a mix.

As it turned out, I was a mixed breed. My German mother's family arrived at Ellis Island as Wagner (meaning wagon driver), while my Irish/English father's family entered as Mac Short. Here was the rub. While Mac is a long-established surname with medieval English and Gaelic origins, it also means "son of." Why my ancestors didn't drop "Short" after leaving the island instead of "Mac" was beyond me.

So thanks to my father and his genes, I was the son of a guy who never grew beyond five foot four. As for me, I hit five six and hadn't measured myself since thirty after reading we lose a quarter of an inch every decade starting at forty. My body might have accelerated the process. Heck, I would have been happy with Wagon Driver after all.

According to my mother, life with my father was great at first. They met in line at the Coney Island Cyclone, a wooden roller coaster in Brooklyn. Poor dad, who was next up, kept reading the four-foot-six height restriction sign until the girl behind him barked, "Come on, shorty, you're not that short."

Love at first sight! My mother loved short men, and my dad loved anyone who appeared interested. Don't get me wrong, my father was good looking, just self-conscious because of his diminutive stature. They rode the Cyclone together and never stopped hanging out. She waited for him to return from World War II to tie the knot.

After several miscarriages, yours truly, Eddie Short, was born, destined to be an only child. They passed down my hazel eyes, dark hair, and olive skin . . . and height, of course. Like I said, I was a mutt. A mutt in desperate need of direction. Where are you, Mom?

"Hi, Eddie."

I recoiled. Oh Christ, not him!

"Sorry I missed your luncheon, but there's been a development."

Two minutes to go, and Mr. Nervous Harry Goldberg was staring at me as though his antipsychotic pill hadn't kicked in. I definitely wasn't going to take his bait.

"Say, Harry, that's OK." The last thing I needed was Goldberg's imaginary friends at my luncheon. He should have taken medical leave last year. Another reason for me to retire. And then it dawned on me why he was standing here: He was next in line for my coveted work space.

I shoved my hand in my cardboard box loaded with my belongings accumulated from the past thirty years and pulled out the last of the pastelito de guayaba, a Cuban cream cheese-and-guava pastry. "Here, Harry, my going-away present to you."

His twitchy eyes darted around before grabbing it and shoving it in his mouth. I held my breath as he sized his new work quarters, surveying my desk, cabinet, and even the carpet, which had been cleaned the week before. A glob of guava dropped to the carpet, and he looked at me, his lips smeared with it. I grabbed a tissue from the box and scooped it up.

"Well, I hope you like your new quarters," I said, smiling. "Good luck."

He nodded, swallowed his last bite, and gazed out the window. "I just hope it's safe," he said in a low voice.

I followed his stare. "Oh, don't worry about the windows. They're hurricane impact."

"Not that. *They* could be out there." Goldberg pointed.

I followed his finger toward the parking lot. "Who?" I asked and turned back to Nervous Goldberg. But he was gone—like his brain lately. How long would he hold onto his new top spot?

I lifted the box off my desk and sighed. It felt lighter without the pastry. Sad, I never took a photo of me with the gang. Oh well, I'll have the memories. Scary thought. I sighed again, realizing every trace of me—Eddie Short—no longer would exist as of tonight. On the other hand, I'd never have to accept another irritating phone call, or pretend to be Mr. Fixit. Nor would I have to decipher e-mails and memos written by the ivory tower folks. A smile spread across my face. Never again would I have to listen to my boss's constant whining about achieving unattainable goals and statistics. There, I said it . . . or, um, thought it.

I surveyed the office one last time. Unless Nervous Goldberg was hiding under a desk, I was alone. I turned out the lights and headed for the elevator. As a typical male, I tended to keep my emotions in check, but I couldn't help sense a void. That feeling picked at me as I drove out of the parking lot. It was the end of a lengthy sentence, yet one I would cherish forever. I searched my rear-view mirror for a sign, but I knew there was no turning back.

Then Kate called.

DECISION TIME—MAYBE

Let's be frank. Anyone older than fifty or even forty who doesn't admit to fantasizing about retirement is either out of touch, has a spouse who barks louder than the boss, has nothing else to live for, or just loves the job. To those last lucky souls, it can't last forever.

Congratulations, your day has arrived. Are you ready? Wouldn't you think submitting your retirement papers is a no-brainer? Wrong! Sure, people dream and talk about retiring—until they're eligible. Remember those fantasies about telling the boss to shove it? Well, they're here. But before walking across the street to retirement, look both ways. Strolling blindly to the other side could be devastating.

And if you've been sucked into watching those ridiculous commercials that hype couples strolling on some exotic island, exploring the North Pole, or sitting naked in a hot tub under the stars outside their McMansion overlooking the Pacific, you must have it to spend it. Oh, right, your tarot card reader forecasted an impending windfall from Uncle Mickey's estate. Return to Earth fast.

Kidding aside, retirement requires thought, thought, and more thought . . . financial, emotional, 24/7 decisions. Will you be ready for Freedom's gate? After all, those fantasies become anticlimactic when retirement finally arrives. Your mantra, "Screw the boss," will be replaced with "Now what?" Remember, those liberating thoughts come with a caveat.

Of course, I had my own retirement fantasies. Like an extramarital affair, I wanted it desperately, thought about it constantly: when, where, how? Fortunately, I didn't have to worry about an affair, considering my game plan and pocketbook included only me and my wife. Then again, some sex would be nice, but that comes later in the story.

So, when retirement was within reach, I thought the decision would be as easy as deveining shrimp. OK, bad example. After all, as an accountant for the Internal Revenue Service, I checked the numbers over and over ad nauseam. I went through every projection, every possible side effect, for answers. In the end, I was even more confused—and that was just the financial part. Then I thought: If my parents survived on their meager savings, were relatively happy, and didn't die of starvation, so could I.

We all have different reasons for retiring, which have little to do with cruises or hot tubs. As for me, I no longer felt effective or satisfied with the job. Every task, memo, projection, and decision I made the last year left me hollow and empty. I was burned out, otherwise known as hitting the wall.

But something foreboding was brewing inside me: my mortality. In the back of my mind, I knew I hadn't dug deep enough to confront the issue. Perhaps I was afraid. I was approaching sixty, not that sixty was old. I'm not vain and admit to coloring my salt-and-pepper mustache, unlike some guys with their trophy wives who refuse to surrender their youth and who look silly with hair dye jobs. I once asked my wife how she would feel if I left her for a younger woman.

"Go for the trophy, Eddie, and you'll end up in last place. Besides, what sexy young woman wants a guy who can only afford Just For Men twice a year?"

My sudden angst on aging persisted. When passing a mirror, I'd check in and greet my father, or at least, what my father would have looked had he lived past fifty, which wasn't a comforting thought. And why was I always reading the obituaries?

To make matters worse, my mother and stepfather passed away within six months of each other when I hit forty. But it wasn't until I lost two close friends, both in their mid-fifties and in seemingly good health, that I truly felt impacted. Like a thief in the night, the Grim Reaper stole my friends' retirement plans. They had prepared for retirement, which only suggested that all the planning in the world was not a guarantee. We can't stop aging and death no matter how many fountain-of-youth products we buy. With my parents and some friends gone, what was in store for me?

I started spending my weekends at the library devouring every book on the subject. I wanted a silver-bullet answer on why, when, and where? But there were none to find. My research came to a screeching halt when the only book I hadn't read dealt with bikers retiring to nudist colonies.

I needed Kate!

KATE

Numb with the information, I approached Kate, who was reading a magazine in the family room, to tell her I'd be in my study finalizing my retirement plans.

She looked up and smiled. "So you're working up the cojones again, huh, Eddie?"

Great encouragement! I held up a pad and pen, and I assured her it was different this time.

Kate nodded. "I seemed to recall you started evaluating your life last year. Are you going to continue where you left off?"

Funny, that wife. Kate never had the opportunity to make an intelligent decision about retirement. During the dot-com bust, my dear wife was forced out of her job when her firm merged with a larger company, sending hundreds of employees to the unemployment line. She landed on her ass with a 201k (half the 401K). There was nothing worse than starting your forced retirement with half of what you'd expected and no social security in sight.

Every time I vacillated about retirement, her bitterness would rear its ugly head. She couldn't understand my reservations, knowing my checking account would be credited once a month, like it or not.

I explained my renewed interest had to do with friends dying off like the plague. "I want a chance to enjoy life before you have to take care of me."

Kate rubbed her stomach. "Don't assume anything, Eddie. You're in better shape. I need to lose five pounds."

I laughed. Kate's mantra was "I need to lose weight." In truth, my wife was in great mental and physical shape, walking at least an hour a day and working the Sunday New York Times crossword puzzle. (I'm a Jumble guy.) She had more hobbies than our local hobby shop. Kate's bottom line: She supported my retirement without hesitation.

Only I wasn't totally convinced. I'm good at reading Kate's body language, and her jaw tightened when we talked about me being home all day. My bottom line: I probably would crimp her lifestyle. You know, like too many cooks in the kitchen. Not that I cook. But Kate needed her space, and our 24/7 togetherness might present a problem—for both of us, actually.

I assured my wife that she looked great and didn't need to lose any weight.

"You want something, don't you, Eddie?"

"What?"

"You don't usually pay me compliments. You want sex or something?"

"No, of course not."

"What, I'm no good anymore? You have a girlfriend?"

"That's not what I meant. Sure, I want sex..."

Kate smiled. "Just kidding. Go to your cave and figure out your life. I'll be here later for sex." She kissed me on the forehead. "if you're a good boy."

"How about . . . ?"

"Go." She pointed. "I know how important this decision is to you. At least you have a chance to plan, not like me. I never had the luxury. I was thrown in the street."

She was so supportive.

"But you don't want to hear my sad story," she continued.

Again. I nodded sympathetically.

"Call me when you want lunch."

"Thanks."

I leaned back into my La-Z-Boy and closed my eyes while mulling the pros and cons.

A knock on the door startled me. "You okay in there, Eddie? It's been over two hours."

My eyes focused on the notepad. Still blank.

Kate gave me one of those looks as I entered the dining room.

"What?"

"You were snoring like crazy. I guess decisions are tiring." She laughed.

As I sat down, I notice my plate was filled with . . . grass. "What's this?"

"Lunch."

"We don't have a rabbit."

"Funny. It's a salad with sunflower seeds, goat cheese, and avocado, sprinkled with alfalfa sprouts. I figured we should start eating right since you're contemplating retirement. What do you think?"

I scratched my head. "I don't know, but shouldn't this be served with something else?"

"Like what?"

"How about a lawn mower?" It must have taken Kate all but three minutes to harvest the grass and wash it before dumping it on my plate.

"Eddie, you have to be open to a healthy lifestyle."

Just what I needed, another mother. "My insurance is paid up, if that's your concern."

She shook her head. "I read how diet plays an important role as we get older. Don't you want to live to a ripe old age?"

I eyed the sprouts. "What's the mortality rate for cows?"

Kate scowled. "Fine, make yourself a peanut butter-and-jelly sandwich."

My eyes lit up.

"With all that sugar and fat, how many years do you think you'll have? And don't ask me to poke your arm with insulin."

"Pass the dressing." She handed me a glass bottle with a funny name on the label. "What's this?"

"We have to go cold turkey. See, it doesn't have any sugar or fat."

I'd settle for cold turkey. I mixed the dressing into my salad and took a bite, then glanced at my wife. "What?"

"You look like a cow chomping on its tongue."

I expected Farmer Gray to bolt through the door and take me to slaughter. I scooped up another fork and munched away. It actually wasn't half bad.

"Did you get all your pros and cons lined up yet?"

"I'm still working on it."

She nodded. "Give me at least one con."

I searched my plate. "Missing juicy hamburgers at lunchtime."

"Come on, Eddie, what's the bottom line?"

She'd been around me too long. "There are more reasons to retire than to continue working."

"That's what you said last year. So when are you putting in your papers?"

I played with my food. "I'm not sure yet."

"I see. Are you looking for the negatives to overcome the positives?"

I shrugged. "It's not that. I want to be sure I'm doing the right thing."

"You want my advice? Forget about the list and put in your papers."

"Just like that?" I said, horrified.

"I guarantee you'll come up with the same answer no matter how much research you do. Here's how I see it," Kate said, striking her index fingers together. "You're one of the lucky ones: You'll be getting a pension. Most people these days don't have that defined benefit thing."

"Defined benefit plan."

"That one. You do because you worked for the federal government. Look what happened to those people at Enron who thought they were going to be on easy street when they retired. They got screwed because of the crooks who ran the place. No job, health plan, nothing. . . . And it's not just Enron. What about those folks whose 401k plans crashed after the dot-com bust? Like mine. Some of those poor souls will have to work until they're ninety, and I'd have to do the same if it weren't for your pension. Want to hear about more casualties?"

I waved my hand in defeat.

"I'm telling you, Eddie, it's the experts who drive us crazy. They're all over the map when it comes to how much money you need in retirement. Some say a minimum of 60 percent of your salary; others advise 80. Which is it, 60 or 80? I wouldn't want to be on the short end of those numbers, or off to work I go."

Kate was clearly enjoying herself. "You know what I think, Eddie? It's not what you make, it's what you spend. You need to determine how much you're going to get from the G-pension and work backward. I did a rough estimate, and you know what? We can do it."

"You worked it out?" I asked incredulously.

"Of course. You might be the accountant in the family, but I pay the bills. So add enough money for food to your plus side."

I started for my study.

"Where are you going?"

I turned. "To get my notebook."

Kate waved me back. "Forget the notebook. It also means we won't be asking Jesse to support us."

I sat, frowned. "Why not? We supported him growing up."

"Because he's got his own bills."

"I recall seeing some of his bills on our desk."

"They were for Christmas presents. He bought them, and we paid the bills."

"In July?"

"His birthday. For chrissake, you treat him like he was your stepson . . . or worse."

Ah, there's our sore spot. The spoiler Kate was, she wanted to shower our only child with gifts. Not that I didn't spoil Jesse. It's just that he needed to understand that money doesn't grow on trees. He once pointed at the Money Store commercial on TV and got excited. I had to tell him they expected something in return.

"Relax, Kate. I'd never ask Jesse for a dime either, even if we had to eat grass for the rest of our lives." I smiled, but she was too focused to return it.

"And as far as your health benefits, we're covered."

"Amen to that."

"That Obama care thing doesn't affect us. God, it's so complicated!"

"Okay, two pluses." If she kept this up, I'd have nothing to do later.

"What else are people concerned about regarding retirement?" Kate asked. "The 'What am I going to do now' thing?" she said, not waiting for an answer.

"I was going to say—"

"There's plenty to do. You just have to find an interest. . . . And I'm not talking about the Internet. God only knows what you'll do online all day when you're home. . . . You might consider taking up golf or some other exercise. And don't tell me you walk. You put on a face every time I ask you to pick up the mail."

I shrugged. "I take out the garbage."

"Twice a week. That ought to keep you in great shape." She softened her tone. "Look, Eddie, all I'm saying is that you need to get up from the computer every now and then. What's going to happen when you're home seven days a week? I don't want you to blow up like Danny Sullivan."

"Who's he?"

"You know, Doctor Keller's receptionist, Donna? Her husband."

"Never met him."

"Me neither. But that's how Donna described him."

I rolled my eyes. "Let me get this straight. You're talking about that mousy woman who keeps asking for my insurance card every time I sign in, even though she's known me for over twenty years?"

"Must be their policy. And she's not mousy."

"Whatever. But that's her?"

"Donna, right."

"She weighs about a hundred pounds."

"What's your point, Eddie?"

"My point is she sees everyone over one-twenty-five as fat. For all we know, her husband might weigh one-thirty."

Kate shook her head. "How did we get here?"

"Where?"

"I was trying to make a point."

"I don't remember. What did it have to do with?"

Kate pressed her temples. "You exhaust me sometimes."

"Okay, I'll join a gym."

"Fitness center."

"That too, if you want."

"They call them fitness centers these days. It's important to get out of the house and exercise a few days a week." She shifted her eyes and tightened her jaw.

"Is this still part of the Donna story?"

She frowned. "Forget it. Keep working until you drop."

I held her hand. "Kate, the last thing I'll do is get in your way. I need my space too."

She attempted to smile. "It's not that I don't want you around, Eddie. It's just that I've been home alone during the day for years, and I like my space. You will too." She smiled warmly. "It doesn't mean we don't like each other."

"I agree."

"Finally, we agree on something." Kate thought a moment. "All kidding aside, Eddie, you want to retire because you sense your mortality. I do too. Here's the thing: What if you died tomorrow? God forbid, but I need to bring home an important point. Your entire adult life would have been your job. You mostly take orders from other people and don't explore your own interests. That's lost opportunity. Why not eliminate the demanding job and the deadlines? And rush-hour traffic? Why not enjoy life while you're healthy?"

She put it so succinctly.

"Put in your papers before death do us part."

INFORMING THE BOSS

Once I finally made my decision, the stress evaporated. I began humming again, often loud and enthusiastic to Kate's dismay. I found myself entering places I never dreamed of, such as the trunk of my car. I sucked out last year's sand pit from Fort Lauderdale beach with the vacuum cleaner, then stowed back everything neatly. From a desk drawer, I cleaned out paid bills and papers from the year of the flood. And when would I take out the garbage without being asked?

Kate worried a brain tumor had caused my odd behavior, but her tight body language relaxed when she realized I was in a good place and that I wouldn't invade her space. She also was relieved the retirement saga was over.

My coworkers hadn't taken my retirements seriously, so they were fairly shocked when I broke the news. I softened the blow by bringing bagels, Cuban pastries, and other goodies for a week.

Employees from every department—some I didn't even know—flocked to my desk like vultures.

I needed to inform my boss, Bill Owens, who worked out of our national office in Washington. With a heavy heart, I drafted a well thought-out letter. My modesty gene short-circuited, and I felt compelled to boast that I had been a faithful soldier and asset for more than thirty years.

However, I decided to e-mail him first. He responded by apologizing for not remembering me. We had met only once, about five years before at a conference in Las Vegas. He requested that I send another e-mail with my name, rank, and serial number, along with a physical description of myself in ten words or less.

I followed through and waited for him to find my personnel file, read it, and get back to me, which he did by phone a few days later, apologizing again for vaguely remembering me from a group picture at The Venetian hotel. Of course, I had more hair, perfect eyesight, and no paunch five years ago, so my updated description hadn't matched the photo. I thought back and described my svelte self back then.

"Oh, now I remember," Owens said. "You were the guy with the jokes. As I recall, you were the center of attention that day, Jerry."

"Eddie," I corrected. "No, that was Eric Munch. He's the comedian. I had the steak."

He chuckled. "That's good, you jokester."

Owens was in his late forties, single, and pleasant, but evidently didn't get out very often.

"You married?" he asked.

Hadn't he read my personnel file? "Thirty-five blissful years." I bet he was smirking on the other end of the line.

"So there's no problem with the missus about you staying home?"

The missus? "She's okay with it. Besides, I won't be home all the time."

"Oh," he said with surprise. "So you're going to seek employment or something?"

"Something like that. Maybe I'll do a few tax returns. I haven't decided yet."

"But you're retiring. You must have a plan."

"Of—of course, I planned."

He was silent a moment until he said, "Doesn't sound like it. What will you do the first year?"

Is this a tax audit? "Stuff."

He cracked up. "You didn't plan, Jerry, admit it."

"Eddie," I corrected again. "I can show you my pre-retirement file."

He laughed. "I believe you, I'm just playing with your head."

Maybe he was right. Maybe I hadn't planned my first year through?

He went on. "It's just that guys think they have retirement down pat, only to discover they're bored after a month."

I looked into the phone. "You a shrink or something?"

He laughed again. "My brother counsels people contemplating retirement. He sees this stuff all the time. It's tragic, you work your entire life, only to get depressed when you retire because you have nothing to do but get old and fat."

"Definitely tax returns! That's what I'll do the first year."

He chortled. "Can't get enough of the tax business, huh?"

My reasons for retiring didn't include sharing them with someone I'd met only once. So instead of revealing I'd hit the wall and lamenting my dead friends, I said, "I love taxes."

"Okay, but make sure you prepare those returns properly. You don't want your clients audited. You'll be a practitioner working the other side of the desk. It could get complicated."

Was that some kind of threat?

Finally, thank God, he asked me to send him my paperwork so he could review it and pass it along.

"It's already in the mail," I said.

"Guess you are serious."

Were we not talking about retirement? "You should have it on your desk by the end of the week."

My sadistic boss hit me with another warning. "I know a lot of guys who put in their paperwork, then get cold feet."

I told him nobody gets cold feet in South Florida.

He liked that one. “Guess you made up your mind.”

Had he been listening?

“’Cause I wouldn’t want you calling me crying that you made a big mistake.”

Did I say I liked this guy?

“Oh, and one more thing, Jerry. Just because you signed the papers doesn’t mean you can start playing solitaire all day on your computer. And keep those personal phone calls to a minimum. You’re still on the clock until the last minute, like in that Jack Nicholson movie. What’s the name of it?”

“About Schmidt?”

“That’s the one. The poor smuck looked lost. Seen it?”

“Three times, but that’s not going to be me. I have a plan.”

“Good for you, Jerry.”

SETTLING IN

On the first Monday of liberation, I descended the stairs like a released tiger. I punched the air and called out to Kate, "How's my girl today?"

My wife's eyes stayed glued to the TV. I joined her on the sofa and leaned back to observe Kate as she watched Live with Kelly and Michael. What a life, sitting around without a care in the world.

"Breakfast?" I asked.

Kate waved me off. "Already had."

I nodded and checked her mug on the table. "More coffee?"

She shook her head quickly, her eyes not inching off the tube.

I shrugged and turned to our old JVC TV to see what all the fuss was about. I snapped my fingers and pointed. "Oh, that's what's his face, you know, the guy who played with De Niro in that movie. Remember?"

“DiCaprio.” Kate answered.

“Right. Great movie. What was the name of it?”

Kate grabbed the remote off the table and froze DiCaprio. “Eddie, I can’t concentrate on the show when you’re talking.”

“Oops, sorry, but it’s not like Jeopardy, you know.”

She produced her usual frown. “This is my favorite morning show, and I don’t like missing any of it.”

I lifted an eyebrow. “C’mon, even the commercials?”

She was about to press the play button when I asked, “Besides, that’s the beauty of DVR. You can watch your shows later on. And you can fly by those annoying commercials at the same time.” Did I sound like a cable salesman?

Kate placed the remote on the table and turned to me. “You’re missing the point, Eddie. You don’t watch Kelly later. That’s why it’s called Live!”

My brain attempted to make sense of her logic.

“You wouldn’t understand,” she said, her shoulders rising.

“Excuse me, but I did graduate from college.”

Kate searched my blank expression. “You need to feel you’re a part of the show. It’s not like Letterman who tapes during the day. Kelly is live!”

Considering I was a C student, I wanted to assure my wife I got that part. Instead, I inched closer and played with her hair.

She pushed my hand away. “I’m not in the mood right now. Can’t you see that?”

"You would be if I was DiCaprio."

Kate pointed at the kitchen. "Go pour yourself some coffee. Better still, make a fresh pot. That should keep you there a while."

I shrugged. "Your loss."

Kate mumbled something about being behind in the show.

I searched for a coffee filter, but after four drawers, I noticed Kate was watching me. "What?"

The remote was back in her hand. She pointed it at me like a PowerPoint presentation. "I've been up since seven watering the plants, reading the newspaper, and eating my breakfast."

"Seriously, that early?"

Another slide from the presentation: "You might want to consider doing the same so you don't waste the entire day."

"Doing?" I let my question hang in the air.

Kate punched the remote as if stuck. "Whatever it is you decide to do that day." She turned off the TV and beckoned me with her finger. "We need to talk."

I filled my cup and entered Kate's air space. I was about to place the cup on the table when Kate dropped her hand underneath. "How many times do I have to tell you to use a coaster?"

I pulled back and steadied the cup. "You mean since I retired?"

Kate snatched a coaster out of the end table. "Since we bought the coffee table ten years ago."

I stared at the square coaster, which displayed a burned picture of Don Quixote. "Didn't we buy these in Spain like twenty years ago?"

She shrugged. "I don't remember. Look, you just retired. You like it, right?"

"Me, it's great. You?"

Kate hesitated. "Maybe not as much as you."

I offered a puzzled look. "You mean it wears off after a while?"

Kate's eyes tightened. "I know this is a novelty for you, Eddie, and I don't mind you finding yourself for a while. But at some point, you might want to consider doing something constructive . . . and respect my morning time."

When I didn't respond, she continued. "Remember when you finally made a decision to retire?"

"Actually, you did."

"With your help. Remember that master plan you were working on?"

"Vaguely."

"About plans to entertain yourself?"

"Sort of."

She smiled. "Well, now would be a good time to fine-tune it. Nothing heavy or written in stone, just daily musings about what you want to do with your life." She eyed my boxer shorts. "For example, you could begin thinking about buying new underwear. Those are worse than some of my rags."

I glanced down. "Oh, this? I couldn't find any in my drawer, so I searched the linen closet."

Kate threw up her hands. "For God's sakes, Eddie, that's a rag!"

I looked down and fingered the material. "Really, it's clean and soft."

Kate shook her head slowly. "And that wasn't the linen closet. How long have you been living here?"

"It looked like a linen closet."

"Since when is our linen stored in the laundry room?"

Was that a trick question?

Kate's face changed to frustration. "I told you yesterday that I was putting your whites in the armoire. Your underwear drawer is broken again. Remember?"

I drew a blank stare.

Kate fidgeted with the remote. "So what do you think?"

I agreed the armoire was a good idea.

"I mean the plan!"

"Right. Yeah, I like it. Any ideas?"

She rubbed her temple. "I need my space."

"Sure, fine. Why didn't you just say so?"

Kate leaned back on the sofa and said she wanted to stick to her routine she'd been following for the past five years.

"You mean like watering the plants, reading the newspaper, and making breakfast for yourself?" I smiled.

She returned my smile. "And Kelly and Michael."

Can't forget Kelly.

"So we need to respect each other's privacy and space."

I nodded and pointed at the tube. "I get it. You want to be alone with them."

"Yes, exactly."

"Seriously?"

"I want to watch my shows in peace and not be hit with a bunch of questions."

I shrugged. "Makes sense to me. So I should be able to watch my telenovelas without you interrupting me, right?"

Kate frowned. "That's different. You translate for me."

I held up a finger. "Yeah, but it's a distraction. Maybe you should learn Spanish."

Kate narrowed her eyes. "You never complained before. Besides, you just want to watch those girls in tight clothes. I swear you make up the dialogue as you go along. . . . How many years of Spanish did you take in school anyway?"

"One semester, but I have a lot of Cuban friends."

Kate shook her head.

"Wanna make out?"

Kate stared at my shorts. "You're impossible, Eddie. And besides, you like sex in the afternoon."

I smiled. “That was before I retired. I have a new plan, remember?”

“We’ll talk about your plan later.”

I headed for my cave with my mug. “I’ll hold you to it.”

She flipped the TV back on. “And change those ridiculous shorts.”

I GET IT!

For a numbers guy, I considered myself a deep thinker. My psychological range crossed many emotional boundaries, and though I didn't always get it the first time, I tended to mull an issue and bring it into prospective. Like when Kate talked about her space.

Since the beginning of our marriage, we'd accepted each other's foibles, though I tested Kate's patience more. Our yin-yang world held us in balance, and we managed to stay on course without petty differences interfering. And while outside forces snuck in, we dealt with them honestly and openly. We respected and like each other. Love was a given.

Kate and I made it through the first day without killing each other. But I knew if this retirement thing had a chance, I would have to make concessions, mainly, allow her to indulge in her structured day. In other words, find my own structure. So after searching my psyche, I understood Kate's desire for space. I also started working through my need for structure and set a course of action. Tomorrow, my alarm clock would go off at seven-thirty sharp. No music, just a cold-turkey buzzer.

The jarring alarm jolted me out of bed, but not before I backhanded it across the room and tripped over the sheets. I managed to shut off the damn thing, swearing about this new experiment, and not happy while squinting in the bathroom mirror light, where I nicked myself shaving. I jumped in the shower, and the warm water soothed me. Why was I doing this? Considering I had no place to go, why not tweak the alarm for an hour later?

Leaving the bedroom, I expected to hear Matt Lauer and his Today crew, but downstairs was quiet. Then I remembered Kate's routine: plants, newspaper, breakfast, and of course, Kelly and Michael at nine. I sung out, "Morning," but Kate didn't reply.

I searched the house and checked the backyard before finding a yellow Sticky on the refrigerator: "Eddie, I'm meeting Maggie. There is plenty of coffee, and I left a bagel in the frig. Probably out for a while. You know Maggie. Love, K."

I frowned. If I had known Kate's plans, I would have delayed my experiment. Balancing a cup of coffee and a toasted bagel, I ambled to the sofa to make room on the table for my breakfast. Between bites, I thumbed through the *Palm Beach Post*, not wasting time on the sports section. Then I tossed it aside and turned on the tube for Kelly to flood my living room. My eyes lingered on her.

I'd never had patience for morning shows, so I started surfing, passing reruns (which I enjoy only at night), news channels, and day-old sporting events. Wouldn't you think I'd be satisfied with more than five hundred channels? My thumb kept pushing until it cramped, and I shut off the tube.

I smiled. It was a typical sunny South Florida day, so I changed into my bathing suit and jumped into the pool. I stared up at a near-perfect sky from my water lounger. Did it get any better than this? I floated for more than an hour, thankful Kate wasn't reprimanding me about sunscreen. Nope, not today.

My wrinkled fingers warned me to clear out, though. I grabbed a towel from the hallway linen closet and left puddles in my wake. After drying off, I dropped the towel on the floor and dragged it back to the sofa with my foot. The sun must have plumped my appetite, so I searched for leftovers in the refrigerator, shifting around Kate's organization. I rubbed my chin and read Kate's note again to see if I'd missed anything. Nope, only coffee and bagels.

I called Kate's cell number. "Having a good time?"

"Great. We're at a charming little outdoor café. You and I should try it sometime."

"Love to. But right now I can't find anything in our charming little refrigerator."

Kate laughed. "We must have finished the leftovers yesterday. I know we have a few eggs left."

I reminded Kate it was lunchtime.

"Gee, Eddie, I don't know what to tell you. Check the pantry. I usually keep a few cans of tuna for emergencies."

"Hold on." I fumbled around the cabinet. Scratch the tuna. In the background, I heard, "Who ordered the cheeseburger?"

"Still there, Kate?"

"Eddie, the food just arrived, so good luck. See you later."

Hello, dial tone. I scoured the kitchen for scraps like some homeless person, settling for both ends of a whole-wheat loaf that had turned funky white. I hesitated, then tossed them in the garbage. I slipped on a T-shirt and shorts, and drove to Taco Bell for a bean burrito at the drive-through.

Famished, I took a wide bite and watched refried beans squirt all over my shirt. Terrific. Now my clean shirt looked like shit—literally. I polished off the burrito with one bite, my throat crying for air. I realized my stomach was going to pay for this indiscretion later.

I reached for my cell phone while negotiating the road and hit the speed dial, only to get a voice greeting. I made two more calls with the same results. The gang must be out chasing taxpayers.

Then I dialed a friend who owned a day school with his wife.

"Say, Jackie, it's Eddie. How's it going?"

"Eddie, hi. It's hectic today, two bus drivers called in sick."

"Too bad. You guys doing anything this weekend?"

A pause. "Are you kidding? I can't think beyond today."

"I can imagine. Is Mickey around?"

"Eddie, he's outside trying to get the kids on the bus. Call back tonight."

Back at home, I checked my e-mails, which had grown like weeds since I signed up for every retailer's newsletter. I hit a few blogs, the news, then back to my e-mail, stopping on a Bass Pro Shop invitation. I followed the menu and wound up in the rods and reels section, where I looked at an ad for a fly-fishing set. Sounded like a fun hobby. I added a reasonably priced combo to my cart, followed the checkout page, and entered my credit card information. Click. "Congratulations, Eddie."

Three o'clock and Kate hadn't returned. I grabbed the remote and started surfing. But after a few minutes, I tossed it on the table and called Kate.

"Having a good time?" I asked.

"Fine, Eddie. What's up?"

"When are you coming home?" I asked like a kid missing his mother.

"Is something wrong?"

I searched the room. "Just wondering is all."

"Maggie's having problems. I'll be a while," Kate whispered.

"What kind of problems?"

"If I could tell you, I would. Later."

"How much—"

Gone. I was about to hop back on my computer when a surge of energy hit me. I found Kate's barbells in the garage and stood in front of a mirror to pump twenty reps in each hand, then another twenty. Damn, these things were heavy. Defeated, I dropped them in place and started playing with the garage door opener, watching the door inch up. I pressed the remote again to close it. One more time. Outside, I noticed a pair of toned legs on a very sexy young woman galloping with two kids in a stroller. I waved, but she had already passed. The next thing I knew, I was power walking after Ms. Tone Legs. Clearly no competition, I slowed down after a few blocks and turned around.

By the time I reached the house, acid reflux had hit me. I searched the medicine cabinet for any resemblance of antacids. Thankfully, I remembered my old office briefcase in the coat closet, the one my boss told me to burn.

Saved. I folded into the sofa and closed my eyes. When I awoke, the house was dark, my stomach had settled down, and there was still no sign of Kate. I called her but got her voice mail. No Kate, no food. Now what?

Like mental telepathy, the phone rang. My savior.

"Where have you been?" I asked, slightly agitated.

"Talking to Jesse. He says hi."

"What's for dinner?"

"Eddie, I'm kind of full. Maggie and I had high tea at the Orchid Tea Room. Want me to pick something up? There's a Taco Bell on the way home."

I checked my shirt. "I'll pass."

"Well, if you think of something soon, let me know."

"Okay. How's Maggie?"

"She's going through a rough patch with Jimmy." A touch of sadness laced her voice. "He's really changed since retiring six months ago. He's not interested in doing anything alone, so he follows her around the house all day. It's clearly not healthy for either of them."

"No kidding."

"He was never like that before. Now he expects Maggie to make lunch every day like his mother. And he never picks up after himself. . . . He even got upset that she was spending the day with me. Can you imagine?"

"What a jerk. Has she told him how she feels?"

"Of course, but he doesn't get it. After years of having the house to herself, she's beginning to feel like a prisoner. She's even talking about leaving him if he doesn't change."

"Get out!"

"She'd have to go back to work, of course. Him too."

Pangs hammered my stomach. My eyes darted about the room.

"You there, Eddie?"

I snapped the towel off the floor, grabbed my breakfast remains from the table, and bounded to the kitchen. I peeled off my stained shirt and sprinted for the laundry room, wondering if I would get back in time to pick up the newspaper. "Where are you now?" I asked out of breath.

MOVIN' OUT

My home always has been my castle. That was especially true in retirement when I could sit around with a second cup of coffee in the morning, or listen to my wife laughing at her favorite shows. And if I was lucky, we'd indulge in a late morning romp.

I had loved living in my house for more than twenty years, full of history and memories, good times like parties and bad times, like a barbecue when a friend suffered a fatal heart attack. Apparently, Murray had consumed too much beef. He was a small-framed guy with a big appetite and would have died sooner or later.

We had a pool, a backyard overlooking a canal, and great neighbors, plus my work commute was less than twenty minutes. It was where our son, Jesse, spent his formative years: the laughter, the crying, and the first girlfriend — Jesse's girlfriend, not mine.

Over the years, those experiences in my psyche bank elicited different emotions, which I find sacred.

So when Kate suggested we should buy a smaller house without even glancing up from her book, I found her callous, and quite frankly, inconsiderate. I mean, I just made one big decision.

Kate and I were like odd bookends on our sofa at three in the afternoon. She sat upright on one side reading a romance novel, and I slouched on the other end engaged in a book on fly-fishing. The gear was arriving in a few days, so I felt obligated to know how to use it.

I closed my book. "What do you mean, too big?"

Kate turned a page. "Big, as we don't need four bedrooms anymore."

"Just like that?" I shot her a look. "Pick up and move?"

Her eyes met mine. "Makes sense, don't you think?"

I dropped the book on the sofa and crossed the room to the sliding doors. I watched a little blue heron leave its nest and glide effortlessly across the canal that led to another canal, eventually emptying into the Intracoastal Waterway. It was faster by car. I turned back to my wife, who must have been savoring a love scene because the words were flying off her lips. "Our canal is perfect for fly-fishing," I said.

Kate stopped lip-syncing, finally closed her book, removed her reading glasses, and sighed. "I've been thinking about moving for a while, Eddie, even before you decided to retire. This is a big house for two people. Heck, we spend all our time in this room."

"What about the bedroom?"

She smiled. "We spend most of the time here."

I glanced around the room. "But we've been living here a long time. Jesse grew up here."

Her smile remained. "And it was great while Jesse was growing up, but he moved out five years ago, and we don't need all this space."

"I recall you telling me you needed more space."

"I wasn't referring to the house, Eddie. We could buy something smaller and still have our privacy."

I turned back to the canal, and my eyes followed a small motorboat. "But I just took up fly-fishing."

Kate patted the cushion to beckon me. "We'll find another place that caters to fly fishermen."

"Like Fort Lauderdale?" I joined her.

She hesitated. "I was thinking northern Palm Beach County."

I frowned. "That's far."

"Maybe, but Broward County is getting too crowded. You said so yourself while you were working. You complained about too many old people on the road during rush hour. Do you realize the population is growing to a point where they're building more condos than single-family homes? High-risers, Eddie."

I grabbed her book and started reading. "Where do you find this stuff?"

She scowled and snatched back the book as though it was the Holy Grail. "Somewhere. Besides, we discussed this in the past, and as usual, you weren't listening."

"I'm listening now." I cupped my hand to my ear. "I like it here and don't want to move. . . . And what about our neighbors and friends? Think how they'll feel when we up and leave." Guilt trip.

Kate touched my face. "We can still see our friends. And as for the neighbors, when was the last time we went out with anyone on this block?"

I thought a moment. "What about the barbeque?"

"That was a block party. Everyone was invited."

I cranked my brain up but came up empty.

"Don't get me wrong." Her voice was conciliatory. "We have great neighbors, but they're mostly young with small children. . . . Let's face it, Eddie, we're the oldest couple in the neighborhood. It's time."

I shook my head. "First retirement, now this. It's too much for me to handle right now."

Kate squeezed my cheek with affection. "You'll get over it. Besides, we don't have to start looking until you're ready. Okay?"

I searched her eyes. "That's fair."

But then her look told me I'd been had. "There's a Realtor I've been talking to, a nice woman with grandchildren who lived in Broward and then moved to Juno Beach after her husband retired. It's quiet and less traffic."

"Juno! That's the other side of the world."

"Funny. It's only an hour from here. She loves it there."

I held up my book. "And I love fly-fishing."

Kate chortled. "Nothing personal, Eddie, but you don't have a clue about fly-fishing. Besides, Juno has lakes, canals, and is closer to the ocean. You love the ocean. You can bike."

"I don't bike, I fish."

"You don't fish, either, but you can do both."

I searched the ceiling, then turned to Kate. "But we just paid off the mortgage. We live free and clear."

Kate sighed. "We can probably find something brand new for less than what we'd sell this place for. That means more money in our pocket."

My ears perked up. "More money?"

She smiled. "Yup."

"A new house means maintenance free for years," I said.

Kate snickered. "When was the last time you fixed anything around here? I'm the maintenance guy, remember?"

"Yeah, but I assist."

Kate rolled her eyes and picked up her book again.

I raised a hand. "Hold on, we're not finished."

Kate lingered on her book before looking up. “Come on, Eddie, you know you want to.”

I folded my arms. “I’m not moving into one of those gated retirement communities. Only old people live there.”

She extended her hand and smiled. “We’re getting old too, but, OK, deal.”

I gazed around and felt like I was losing an old friend. “I’m gonna miss this place.”

Kate squeezed my hand gently. “Me too, honey, but it’s time.”

I smiled wistfully and thought of our son. “Oh my God, Jesse is going to be so upset. You’ll have to call him, Kate. I don’t want him crying to me over the phone.”

“I already did. He thinks it’s a great idea. Just think, we’ll probably see more of him since he’ll be staying over some weekends.”

I scowled. “What a minute, you talked to Jesse before me?”

“I always talk things over with Jesse first. He’s more open-minded.”

I shook my head in defeat.

Kate snuggled up to me and nibbled at my ear. “They say it’s more romantic in Juno Beach.” Then she talked sexy in my ear, probably lines from her romance novel, and touched me in places that got my attention. Sold! “Call your Realtor friend and tell her we’re interested.”

She nipped my neck. “I already did.”

ST JOSEPH, CAN YOU HELP ME?

Our move was on hold. You might ask why, given that almost every For Sale sign planted in our neighborhood the past month had been removed.

Two months ago, we signed a sales agreement with a broker who assured our house would be sold in days. Liar.

I can't tell you how often my nose pressed against the windowpane searching for a warm body to appear on my walkway. The neighbors must have thought I was some kind of pervert. I developed blisters on my feet from pacing, waiting for one lousy buyer to make an offer.

Kate turned our place into a "House of the Month," like she had entered a contest. Everything was immaculate, and I was afraid to move for fear of disturbing the "décor." Every morning, she would buy flowers at the supermarket, and on occasion, white lavender or some other fragrance that killed my sinuses. For whom? No one ever showed up.

When I called my broker, he was either on the other phone or out chasing clients. That's a good one. When I finally tracked down the Almighty, he told me not to worry. "Soon, Mr. Short, soon." Liar.

Like I had nothing better to do than stand outside my front door staring at the sign, wondering if a subliminal message read, "Don't stop here." Even more insulting, drivers in moving vans waved to me on their way to every address but mine. Despite an active real estate market, our house had 666 written all over it.

I should have known better when deal-lover Kate signed us up with a discount broker who she heard could save us thousands in commissions.

We should have researched it before buying into the idea. Then I would have known the average full-service Realtor would rather be buried alive than share a commission with a discount broker in a healthy real estate market.

So we sat around and waited. And waited.

I hadn't touched my fly-fishing book in a month. Now I was reading self-help books on selling your house in one easy lesson. Liars.

After talking to her Realtor friend in Juno Beach, Kate delivered good news. "St. Joseph will sell it for us."

I gave her a look as though she had lost her mind. "Not the St. Joseph."

She nodded. "That one."

I rubbed my chin, mulling my wife's apparent desperation. It didn't make any sense. "I thought he was a carpenter."

"He is, silly, but St. Joseph is also the patron saint of the home and family."

I rolled my eyes. "Let me get this straight, you're telling me that St. Joseph, the father of Jesus, is in charge of selling homes? What, like a side business?"

She laughed. "All I'm saying is that St. Joseph will come through for us."

I frowned. "Gee, I don't know, it kind of sounds a little sacrilegious."

"We're desperate!"

"We're not even that religious."

A wide smile. "That's the beauty of St. Joseph, Eddie. You don't have to be religious. In fact, atheists use him. So do real estate brokers."

"Apparently not ours. So what, we call him or something?"

"We bury him."

"Whoa, what would the Pope think?"

Kate assured me the Pope would approve. "The way it works is we bury a plastic statue of him in the front yard."

I scratched my head, still doubtful. "And where do we find St. Joseph?"

"He's in every Christian store, all shapes and sizes. Heck, I'm sure he's sitting on one of the shelves waiting for us right here in town. I think it's called The Christian Store."

"Very apropos. What are we waiting for? I'll drive."

"Gee, Eddie, I have too much to do. How about you go?"

"I can't go alone. I mean, I never did this before. Besides, they'll figure out I'm desperate."

"You are."

Evidently, other people were using discount brokers because St. Joseph was nowhere to be found at the store. So I searched every town within a ten-mile radius.

Nothing, except St. Joseph holding baby Jesus. No way, I wasn't burying Jesus. So I approached the last shop, where a young ethereal-looking woman with a warm smile asked if she could assist me.

"St. Joseph?" I coughed.

She pointed at the opposite wall. "What size?"

Size? "Well, I don't really know. What do you suggest?"

"That depends on the purpose."

I swallowed hard. "To bury him."

"Oh, you're selling your house." Her face lit up the store.

I nodded sheepishly then followed her to the shelf filled with every Christian statue known to man. I couldn't tell one from another. She held up a nine-inch white plastic statue, presumably St. Joseph. “Perfect for burying.” She handed it to me. “It’s made in the good old U.S.A.”

“I’m definitely patriotic. And religious.”

Miss Sunshine informed me that people who bury St. Joseph are able to sell their house within seven days, according to legend.

Seven! I slapped down a dollar and bolted for the door. Couldn’t wait to show Kate.

“Mister?”

Please don’t tell me you made a mistake. I turned. “Yes?”

“How about a prayer card? It’s only a quarter, and it reinforces your request. I’ve had good results.”

Definitely a prayer card. I dug in my pocket for change.

As I raced for my car, St. Joseph slipped out of my hand. My eyes darted about as I scooped my favorite saint off the ground and shoved him in my pants pocket. I got in the car and called Kate. “I got him, I got him!”

“Oh, that’s great, but I think we have a buyer.”

I felt the smooth plastic in my pocket. “What are you talking about? We haven’t even buried him yet.”

“Well, he must have known you were looking for him because a nice young couple with two children stopped by after you left, and they love it.”

“Catholic?”

"Jewish. By the way, I found out we could have gotten a St. Joseph kit online. It comes with a prayer card."

I leaned my head against the wheel. What was the store's return policy?

"Hurry home, we'll celebrate."

CLUTTER ME NOT

Death, divorce, and taxes—couldn't help throwing in the last one—were a few of life's stressors. Kate would add living with me, but I believed that was in jest, although lately she kept bringing up how Jimmy and Maggie—probably more Maggie—were coping with the trials of Jimmy's retirement.

I had assumed retirement life would be one long uninterrupted vacation. Then Kate decided to move, a sixty-mile schlep to a new neighborhood, leaving behind family and friends.

On top of that, I had to fit a twenty-seven hundred square-foot house into an eighteen hundred square-foot townhouse. Try explaining that to Kate.

And try telling her we don't have clutter. We'd lived in this house more than twenty years and accumulated thirty years of crapola. It reminded me of a St. Vincent de Paul Thrift Store: vacations trinkets, tchotchkes, holiday gifts received but never used, or re-gifted, and other people's crap from garage sales that had stockpiled in every closet of every room. I didn't have a problem tossing out 90 percent of the junk. Not so my wife.

Kate and I decided to work in tandem; I think she wanted to keep an eye on me. We started with the upstairs bedroom and worked our way downstairs to the smallest closet—my cave. The only saving grace was that we didn't have a basement, but we did have a two-car garage, which silly me, I thought was meant for cars.

We began in the master bedroom closet, where I should have been entitled to a third of the space. That was fair, considering about a fifth of the clothes were mine. I dumped my shirts and slacks into two cardboard boxes. I already had given Goodwill anything resembling work clothes and called it a day. Kate, though, struggled on her first box, agonizing over which dresses to donate.

"What?" she asked glumly.

"You look like you're about to cry. They're only clothes." I pointed at the blue dress in her hands. "Quite honestly, I don't remember you ever wearing that."

She shot me a look like I'd killed a family pet. "You wouldn't understand, Eddie, you're a man."

Well, at least we agreed on that. "When are you going to wear it again?" I glanced at the maze of dresses hanging like soldiers on the rack.

She touched the silk fabric with tenderness. "You never know."

"That's my point, Kate. You'll never wear it again, and you *know* it."

She glared. "This dress has history."

So do many at the Smithsonian. I wanted to ask what year or era, but her glare held me off. My chin nodded to my two boxes on the floor. "It was easy for me. I don't hold on to things like you do."

Kate burst into tears. "Is that what you think of me? Just something you might not want to hold on to one day? So when I get sick and you don't want me anymore, you'll discard me like this dress."

"Huh?"

"You're just like Manny Cruz," she said, wringing her dress like it was my neck.

"Who the hell is Manny Cruz?"

"On your telenovela, he's leaving his wife for a new dress."

I scratched my head. "Manny Cruz is the attorney. You're thinking of Eduardo Romano. And he's not leaving her for a dress. He's leaving her because she's a ball breaker."

"Whatever. I need my space right now."

I shook my head. "I think it's your hormones, Kate. You gotta ask your doctor to increase the dosage."

She gave me another Kate look. "It's always about hormones, Eddie. It's never about understanding."

I glanced at one of Kate's corners where office uniforms were squeezed in next to sweaters. She probably last wore them more than five years ago. "Do you really think you can still fit into those uniforms, much less want to wear them out to dinner?"

Kate dropped the dress, whipped off her shorts, and tugged herself into a uniform. It took two tries to zip up. "There, Mr. Smart Ass, I can still fit into it."

I considered saying she needed to cut back on bread, but that would be suicide. Instead, I told her I'd be in the next room.

I angled myself, sucked in my stomach, and stepped inside the dark guest bedroom closet. I slithered to one corner to feel around for the light switch. Stepping back to draw in air, I was transported back in time: Jesse's kid clothes, Kate's wedding dress, coats we'd never wear again, and … platform shoes?

I stormed back into our bedroom where Kate was still in uniform mulling over the damn dress. "What the hell do you expect to do with all that crap in there?"

She hurled the dress at me. So much for sentimentalities. "Get out of here, Eddie! Can't you see I'm in mourning?"

"Listen to me, Kate. We're moving into a smaller place and have to be practical."

"You're too damn practical! I can't do this."

"Move? But you're the one—"

"Don't you get it? I'm leaving behind part of my life. I can't cut the umbilical cord."

There was more to moving than making dress decisions. Kate obviously was suffering from separation anxiety. I approached, but she stuck out her hand. "Go back to what you were doing."

I dropped my hands. "Look, I can't make a decision without you. Most of those things are yours."

"Just get rid of whatever you want. I don't care anymore." She turned her back to me.

I thrust into the time warp again and was about to toss Jesse's blue suit on the bed when I stopped. I held it up and breathed in a faint scent of Old Spice, which I had splashed on him when he was a ring bearer for a wedding. I sighed. The suit lasted longer than their marriage. I laid it on the bed and found my old cashmere overcoat. Reminiscing about the good old days in New York, I slipped it over my T-shirt and shorts. In the pockets, I found a pair of black leather gloves and a theater ticket stub. I tried on the gloves and caught myself in the mirror, searching for the reflection of a younger man. Smiling wistfully, I felt the history in this old friend.

Back in our bedroom, I lay in wait for Kate to turn around. She had changed into the dress, and we burst out laughing when she noticed me.

She touched the cashmere. "You still look good in that thing, Eddie."

And Kate looked terrific in her blue dress. I remembered she wore it for our twenty-fifth anniversary party. "You look the same." I meant it.

I removed my coat and gloves, and we embraced. "I really do understand how you feel, Kate."

Her eyes met mine, and she smiled before kissing me passionately on the lips. "Let's celebrate our twenty-fifth again."

Hello, Juno.

After waving goodbye to our movers, I turned and faced our new home, a Mediterranean-style townhouse. My brain was too weary to appreciate the style or new construction, and I was too numb to be wistful about my old place. Standing alone, I panned the empty street. No movement, no neighbors. Just us.

Inside, Kate was unpacking. Fortunately, we finally resolved that less was best and held a memorial service for everything left behind. We realized we still had memories and that our remaining possessions would be just another part of our lives going forward.

Before moving, Kate and I played a game of scenarios about our life in Juno Beach to help quell our anxiety. How far would we have to travel for a pizza and movie? Would the local newspaper have a decent entertainment section? Would the librarian be as helpful as our last one? Kate wondered about a walking trail. I wanted a place to fly fish.

Our hearts were still in our old house, but we also accepted it was no longer ours and that we needed to make Juno Beach a home that reflected who we were. Jesse, who lived two hours south of us would be visiting us occasionally on weekends, and we wouldn't have to worry about him eating and running. Now we'd eat, talk, and watch some TV before he put us to bed.

Kate set up the portable CD player and was listening to one of Vivaldi's Four Seasons. She'd been in a better mood since we solved the clutter business.

"Hey," I said. She turned to me. "We're gonna be okay."

Kate's smile told me she felt the same.

RUNAWAY DECORATOR

Kate and I settled in quickly, considering our daunting task. We tripped over boxes, furniture, and each other, forging ahead room by room until the last piece of ourselves was in place. Outside, we stacked up a mountain of cut-up cardboard boxes for the garbage people.

Satisfied, we explored the area the following week, lunching at an outdoor café on the beach, catching a few matinee movies, and of course, visiting our town library. We didn't even have time to cook, so we ordered Chinese takeout and pizza delivery—the driver couldn’t find us for more than an hour.

Kate had picked up temporary paper window shades for privacy despite no signs of civilization, evidence of Kate’s impulsiveness to be the first to move into our subdivision. We discovered the next house wouldn’t close for at least another week, consequently delaying phone and cable services. That meant the television screen remained black while our cell phone charges piled up.

Our townhouse felt tiny but cozy, not cramped as I had feared. We settled into our old routine of mostly reading—me back in my fly-fishing manual. But we didn't hesitate to fool around like teenagers, christening one room after another. We had only five rooms, though, and given my delicate back, we skipped the kitchen table. Kate also banned the two-and-a-half baths—no explanation given. My serotonin level hit an all-time high because my voracious appetite for quickies was more than Kate could handle.

"I'm trying to read, Eddie," she would plea. Or, "Not now, Eddie, it's four o'clock in the morning!"

I admit soon after the sale of our house, my stress levels took a nose dive, and consequently, my appetite for sex shot up. But at my age, my libido finally leveled off, so I got up at night only to pee. One night, I woke in a start forgetting we had moved. A pee is always comforting, so I paid a visit to the bathroom and continued down the hall into the guest bedroom where I glanced at the window. I swore the reflection from the moon cast a shadow of my father's face, like he was smiling at me. I appreciated the small gift, given my father rarely smiled, especially toward the end of his short life. I rubbed my eyes, and he was gone.

By the end of the second week, we decided to invite over friends, but everyone was busy, including Jesse, who was on a business trip to L.A., and decided to take off a week for a drive to the wine country. We got antsy but continued our routine.

During our third week, Kate sprung it on me. “We need to decorate.”

I should have seen it coming from the magazines spread across the family room coffee table. “Say again?”

My feet were resting on one of the magazines, and I was sipping a Francis Coppola’s merlot. I was a big fan of his movies. Kate placed her glass on Don Quixote’s head and yanked the *Decorating* magazine from under my feet. Thanks. She thumbed through it and shoved it in front of my nose. “What do you think?” she asked with a wide smile.

“OK, it’s a living room.” I shrugged, not wanting to give so much as a spark to her apparent master plan.

“Not just a living room, a newly decorated living room. Look around, dear, we just bought a new house and still have the same old furniture.” She frowned. “Look at this room, Eddie!”

I looked around and squeezed my shoulders. “I admit the walls could be dressed up with a few prints, but otherwise the room looks fine to me.”

Kate narrowed her gaze. "To you, maybe, but you're not an expert. Besides, the furniture is over ten years old. We can't entertain our friends like this. What would they think?"

I scratched my head. If this was a hidden agenda, why did we move all this heavy furniture when we could have donated it to Salvation Army, gotten a charitable deduction, and saved a bundle on the move? "And when did you get this idea?"

"You know me, I'm always thinking."

I rolled my eyes. "You watch HGTV."

She tossed *Decorating* on the table two inches from Coppola's merlot. "My friends appreciate my input. Janet loved the way I decorated her bedroom. Now she and Sammy have more … quality time."

"Maybe you should consider decorating our bedroom," I said then regretted my comment

"You're going to eat those words."

I waved my hand and attempted a conciliatory tone. "So what's your plan, dear?"

Kate glanced around, nodded. "We need to rearrange a little."

Nothing was ever "a little" with Kate. "Like?"

She started pointing like a pro. "First of all, this entertainment unit needs to go, which means we have to match the replacement with a new sofa." She crossed the room with authority. "We'll have to add a few slipper chairs over here." She tapped the coffee table with her big toe. "We need to replace this too."

I jumped up to protest, even though I knew it was futile. “That’s the whole room! And how come you didn’t mention my HDTV with all the bells and whistles?”

Another point. “Too expensive, your forty-two-inch Sony is just fine.”

I smacked my forehead. “How much is this going to cost, Ms. Interior Designer?”

She met my eyes and smiled. “Can’t tell yet, but I’ll throw in my services gratis.”

Defeated, I folded back into my chair.

“Come on, Eddie, it’ll be fun.”

“It’ll be expensive.” I shook my head, attempting to add up the damage.

“And fun. Look, we don’t have anything else to do. I mean, we’re retired.”

Right, retired and heading for broke. “I guess I can live with that.” I got up to seek solace in my cave.

“Wait, I’m not finished. Wait till you see what I have planned for the other rooms.”

I had a runaway decorator on my hands.

NO INTEREST FOR TWENTY-FOUR MONTHS!

The following week, after consuming every decorating book and magazine ever written, Kate, ammunition in hand, grabbed me on her way out the door. "I need your support, Eddie."

Right, like she would listen to me.

"No payments for twelve months." She pointed excitedly at a store flier as we got into the car.

I nodded indifferently.

"Look, no payments or interest for twenty-four months!"

"Miss the last payment, and it's called usury."

Kate placed the newspaper ad on her lap and turned to me. "Come on, Eddie, I thought you liked deals."

My eyes remained on the road. "You like deals. I like when merchandise falls off a truck."

Kate shook her head. "I thought this was going to be fun."

Attempting to tune out her enthusiasm, I recalled how my mother dragged my stepfather to every store at the mall until he surrendered to exhaustion. She then dropped him off in the Sears's furniture department where other old-timers waited around on chairs and sofas, sometimes falling asleep in the bedding department. It was like a day-care center for the elderly. He actually made a few poker buddies. That never would be me, I swore.

But when we arrived at a department store in West Palm Beach, I followed Kate to a makeshift bedroom. "Wait for me here," she said.

I shrugged. "Sure." Anything was better than following my wife around every aisle like a stray dog looking for food. She turned to leave, then paused. "And behave yourself. Not like the last time."

That was more than ten years ago! We were in a department store, maybe Sears or Macy's, I don't remember, but I didn't want to be there. Kate wanted company, why I didn't know, because as soon as we arrived, she told me to meet her back at this spot in an hour. Right. So after an hour of strolling every department, except one, I drifted into forbidden territory: the lingerie section. A smiling, young, beautiful woman, someone I'd expect to shop at Victoria's Secret, approached me to ask for assistance. I looked down at my shirt for a nametag. When I explained I was a customer once removed, she said she wanted a man's opinion. Any man apparently. I searched the department for Kate and smiled. “I’d be glad to.” After all, how could I refuse a damsel in distress?

Then Kate spoiled the fun when she found us huddling around a teddy discussing cup sizes. She grabbed my arm, the teddy releasing from my hand. “I said meet me at the exit in an hour, not the play room.”

“Eddie, are you in one of those zones again?”

I blinked, smiled back. “I’ll be good.” And I was until I checked out a queen bed. I dug my butt around on it and aimed my head at the pillow. The next thing I knew someone was tapping me on the shoulder.

“Sorry to bother you, but are you okay?”

I smiled. An angel from heaven? “Must have dozed off.” I yawned.

“Can I?” A thirty-something blonde with a tight ponytail was motioning. She wore a tank top with plenty of saline underneath.

My head jerked around for Kate. Not again. “Uh, sure.” I shifted to give her a wide berth. “I’m not a salesman, though.”

“Oh, that’s OK. Just want to get a feel.”

Feel?

Ms. Ponytail smiled and proceeded to bounce, digging in. “You like?”

My eyes drifted north and I nodded.

“Me too. It’s hard, but not too hard. You like hard?”

Hard?

I nodded again. “Uh, very.”

“How about you roll over on your back?”

Huh? And then I realized I always do as I’m told. I stared at the ceiling thinking pure thoughts.

The mattress hadn’t moved, definitely a hard bed. She was so close, the scent from— honeysuckle?—filled my nostrils. She slithered closer and draped her arm over me, snuggling up. I froze.

“This is perfect,” she said, giggling.

“A-hah,” was all I could force out.

“He’s a bit bigger than you.”

That caught me off guard.

“Taller, I mean. My boyfriend is slightly taller, but you’re about the same size.”

I felt a whole lot better.

“Hey!” a deep, threatening voice barked. “What the hell is going on?”

Definitely not Kate. Oh, well, the manager caught us. But then, “

Who the hell are you with, Ariel?”

Definitely not the manager. I wasn’t Ariel, so apparently the woman whose arms were locked on me was.

“That’s Diablo, his nickname. I thought he was in the sports department,” she whispered. “This was supposed to be a surprise.”

Great, the devil was upset. “I don’t believe it is anymore,” I said.

She sat up. "Oh, well, his loss." She got out of bed. "Diablo, it's not what you think."

I sat up and waved at Diablo, who indeed was bigger and taller, and probably would kick my ass if I didn't bolt out of there.

He glared at me. "I'll have your ass fired, scumbag." His voice echoed through the department.

Great, now he thought I worked here.

"He's not a salesman," Ariel said. "He's just a nice old man trying to help me out."

Old? "It's true. I'm waiting for my wife to show up. She walks with a cane and . . ." I needed to milk this.

His eyes softened. "Oh, well, thanks mister."

"Still in bed, I see." Kate's arms were filled with bags—without a cane. "Gonna introduce me?"

Diablo smiled at my wife. "He'd make a great salesman."

Ariel agreed. "Come on, Diablo, we have more shopping to do." She slipped me a final wink.

Kate dropped her bags and climbed on the bed with me. "Very comfortable . . . and hard, don't you think?"

Hard?

She smiled. "Wanna see what I bought?"

COUPONS, RAIN CHECKS, CROWDED AISLES!

OK, I'll admit, the decorating business went well, with Kate focusing on one room at a time. Since we didn't need a new bed—I never went into the whole Ariel/Diablo thing, for fear of being reprimanded for initiating too friendly an atmosphere—Kate began with the family room. Her color schemes perfectly matched the new furnishings. Quite honestly, the room took on a stylish look with a more updated trend—without sacrificing cost, of course. I was still waiting for my new TV, though.

As Kate moved on to one of the guest bedrooms, I caught up with my nothing-to-do business until she knocked on my cave door to ask for a favor. A favor generally meant I got stuck with one of Kate's low-priority chores, such as grocery shopping.

The request sounded reasonable, but we'd divvied up the household chores years ago, and she lost on that one. She actually found grocery shopping therapeutic. Can you imagine?

Armed with a fanny pack containing a concise list, her airline points' MasterCard, and neatly trimmed coupons, Kate stayed focused, seldom veering unless she spotted a deal. Yet, she was capable of spending like a drunken sailor. To her, every coupon was gold that would find its way to the bank. It all made perfect sense—to her. Unfortunately, that strategy sucked even more from our bank account.

To me, grocery shopping was a necessary evil, like "Will work for food." Nothing was more annoying than negotiating a shopping cart down an aisle against a charge of strollers, walkers, and motorized carts. Or, slithering pass shoppers comparing brands, prices, and calories in the middle on the aisle. And forget about the flatulent sufferers who refused to be discreet.

Unlike Kate, I had little patience for cutting out tiny newspaper coupons like they were works of art. In fact, my mother once admitted I was almost held back in kindergarten because of my lack of aptitude for art projects. The teacher also expressed concern that I had a propensity to use only black crayons in my coloring book. Years later, we discovered I was colorblind, to my mother's relief.

My lack of interest in cut and paste changed on the job when I prepared documents on the computer, but that was due more to laziness.

On occasion, Kate and I would exchange chores when it became impractical. Once, while running late from work, she asked me to pick up a cooked chicken dinner. I was tired and cranky—from work—and just wanted to get home. I had missed lunch because of a last-minute report on a tax relief provision after hurricanes. Not a good move, considering I'm hypoglycemic. After grabbing a barbeque chicken, I dashed to the express line and watched the cashier scan groceries for an elderly woman holding a wad of coupons.

I shook my head as the cashier announced to the world, "This coupon has expired."

"This isn't October 31?" the elderly woman asked.

"It's November 2, ma'am," the high schooler said to no one in particular.

"No grace period?"

The cashier rolled her eyes at me. "No, ma'am." Her attitude assured me she could give two shits that the line had grown like weeds. She probably was working until the store closed, which the way we were going, would end with me.

The cashier attempted to validate another coupon and shook her head. "You didn't buy Pampers." The woman searched frantically through her groceries. "Gotta be in here somewhere."

I clenched my fists and thought about paying for the fucking Pampers that didn't exist. Instead, I grabbed a Hershey's bar from the rack and devoured it in two bites.

The old woman caked with makeup turned to me. "Must have forgotten to add it to my cart."

The cashier took that as a, "You got me," and totaled the bill.

Ms. Cottonball Head started mumbling and digging through her purse until her hand surfaced with a credit card, which I prayed hadn't expired.

"It didn't go through," Miss Courtesy said.

The old woman made another attempt, and I noticed she was sliding the card in backward.

"Here, let me help." I reached for her card with chocolate smeared on my lips. But the woman screamed at the top of her eighty-something lungs as if I was robbing her, prompting the guy behind me to spew expletives. I pulled back sheepishly, licked my lips, and searched the floor.

Naturally, Kate got home before me.

"Where the heck have you been, Eddie? I'm starved."

"Attempted robbery at the supermarket."

Back in my cave, Kate followed through on my instinct: "Eddie, I left the grocery list on the kitchen table." She smiled and thanked me before turning to leave. "Oh, and don't forget the coupons."

"Right, coupons."

"And make sure you get a rain check for anything on the list they ran out of. Enjoy."

I nodded. “Yes, dear.” I checked my watch. Perfect timing for grocery shopping. I didn’t do fanny packs, so I shoved the list and coupons into my shorts’ pocket and took off. The neighborhood was becoming active as moving vans lined up in front of the remaining empty houses. Some of the new residents caught me driving down the street and waved with smiles. I did my neighborly part by rolling down the window and honking my horn.

I generally shopped on my time so it was no surprise that I found a spot in front of our new Winn-Dixie supermarket. I studied the list, which my dear wife had categorized with the corresponding coupons. Once inside, I placed the ammunition on top of the cart and ambled about like I owned the place. It was an exceptionally quiet day, so I figured I should be out in less than twenty minutes.

Kate’s coupons promised a free loaf of bread, a store brand bag of potato chips, and Armour crackers if I spent at least $25. With every item I placed in the cart, my accounting brain kicked in. I soon arrived at the quota, then thirty dollars, and before long, fifty. The roll call stopped at about fifty-eight and change, so I picked up the bread and chips before proceeding to the cookie section for the crackers. This was normally a tough aisle to negotiate, but I didn’t encounter young mothers with Hummer carts, or a dozen kids running up and down high on sweets from the shelves.

Today was my day, so I wandered about searching for crackers by Armour. I found Nabisco, Keebler, and other brand names, but no Armour. I wasted a good five minutes and was about to leave when an elderly couple invaded my turf. The guy, wearing a New York Yankee ball cap at a forty-five degree angle and holding a similar coupon in his hand, trudged toward me, his wife barking orders. Our eyes met, and I could tell he was a broken man.

"Crackers, right?" I asked with sympathy.

He nodded, thumbed back at his wife. "Already been down this aisle three times. Can't find the crackers."

"Me neither," I said.

"Driving me crazy," he whispered as he passed. I glanced at his wife, who gripped the cart with both hands and appeared ready to plow over him.

"I'll check with someone," I said.

I found a produce guy who was feeling up a few peaches.

"Excuse me," I said evenly, not wanting to ruin the guy's fantasy. "I can't seem to find these crackers." I waved the coupon in his face.

He dropped a peach, dusted it off with his apron, and placed it in the bin. He eyed the coupon. "Crackers?"

"Armour." I shrugged. "I searched the cookie aisle with no luck, and there's a guy who might get run over if he doesn't find them, or laid if he finds them before dark."

The produce guy smiled. "You're in the wrong department. Those crackers come with lunch meat."

"Lunch meat?"

"You obviously don't have kids."

I shook my head. "My bank owns him."

He laughed. Must be boring in the produce section. "Try the pre-wrapped cold-cut department. Aisle 12."

My ice cream was melting, and the milk was losing two days off the expiration date, so I hightailed to 12. I nosed each item until I found the Armour package and savored a smile. Then I heard shuffling feet and knew the old guy had reached his destination. I turned. He was alone but not happy, the coupon limp in his hand.

I waved. "Found it!"

His eyes sparkled as he hustled over like a tackler on steroids. I pulled the package off the ring and realized it was the last one. Uh-oh. I had two choices: screw the old man or request a rain check.

I pictured myself in twenty years and offered him the package. "You're in luck." I smiled.

His arthritic hand grabbed the package like it was gold and studied it for a few moments before glancing up. "What the hell is this?"

I attempted to read the label between his gnarled hands. "Looks like a fake lunchbox with a couple of slices of turkey and cheese." I looked closer. "And a Butterfinger bar for dessert. Yummy."

"Yeah, but where are the frigging crackers?"

I shrugged. "Hidden between the meat and cheese?"

He wiped his forehead. "Yeah, but how many crackers can fit in this thing?"

I was tempted to tell him I didn't work for Armour. Instead, I tried to take the package to read the contents, but he jerked his hand back.

I held up my hands in defense. "Enough for each slice, maybe five."

He sneered. "I've been roaming this store for five crackers?"

"Five free crackers."

He glared. "What are you, a smart guy or something?"

I could have reminded him that I wasn't the one shoving the cart up his ass, but he looked too spent.

"It requires refrigeration," I said and left him staring at his freebie.

HITTING A WALL!

Five months into my retirement, I found myself sprawled on the sofa waiting for something to happen. My eyes stopped on one of Kate's magazines on the coffee table. Where did that come from? I stared at the cover photo of a guy holding a putter on a golf course, his face drawn as though he had just missed a clincher shot. The headline read, "Men Losing the Retirement Game."

I rifled through the magazine for the article. On page twenty-six, the poor guy faced me again, this time his shoulders sagging, his face crying out for help.

"I can't do this anymore," the article began. Not a good opening. After a few paragraphs, it became painfully clear many of my fellow retirees were in trouble. The article said a significant number of men were less satisfied with life after a year into retirement and had greater expectations for their fourth act.

The female writer suggested that men's planning generally starts and ends with finances, such as focusing on how much money needed for a cruise instead of ensuring he has enough activities to fill a day. The more free time, the more potential for boredom. And boredom spelled a negative health impact. For a man retired in his sixties with perhaps a quarter of his life left, that was a long time to be bored.

A survey sidebar said some men were more positive about their future: golf fanatics and weekend fixer-uppers. These wishful thinkers swore golf and those ever-to-do projects would satisfy them until their Almighty called for a different kind of project.

I snickered. Projects? While I hadn't dismissed those other activities, I doubted if the weekend projects I had put on hold for twenty years could provide meaning and purpose for the next twenty. Or even get off the ground. As for golf, I wasn't into it, but even so, three to four days a week on the greens could only last so long. One, I'd run out of money, and two, who the hell wanted to search for lost balls all day? And why hadn't the article addressed hip problems?

It closed with an apocalyptic ending. Without enough structure, many men would have to return to the workforce, or suffer grave mental and physical consequences. (Apparently, women somehow escaped this insidious curse.)

Bottom line: No activities equaled boredom, and boredom equaled mental and/or physical stress.

Oh boy, what a fun article! Had Kate planted it near my TV remote?

I thought about my mother and stepfather's traditional marriage. They were truly devoted to each other, but simple things mattered in their generation. My stepfather espoused that men went to work, returned home, ate dinner, and went to bed. If I was lucky, I'd start all over again the next day.

Not very high expectations. And retirement became a simple extension for that generation. As a baby boomer, I expected to become more active and productive in retirement, though, quite frankly, I hadn't figured out how.

Kate's lifestyle had made it seem like a snap. After all, she was seemingly happy with her solitary projects. In fact, her only complaint was she didn't have enough time in the day. But as my retirement limped along, I realized I wasn't like her. Not interested in sports or projects, I got excited connecting with people. And the only connection I got these days was with the Internet. Quite frankly, I was feeling lost.

I searched the ceiling for answers. When they didn't appear, I aimed the remote at my new fifty-inch Sony flat-panel HDTV. Kate finally consented, tired of watching me pout all day. Agitated by the article, I throttled the remote, finally landing on some cooking channel where a smiling Giada De Laurentiis was creating chicken piccata. (I loved her grandfather's movies.) I was about to lift my half-eaten turkey on rye off the coffee table when another woman blocked Giada, this one not smiling.

I blinked hard. "Hi. Where'd you come from?"

Kate's arms were folded. "The sofa is going to have a permanent outline of your body like a crime scene."

I wanted to laugh, but Kate still wasn't smiling.

She continued. "And, I might add, those shows aren't going to help you slow down your appetite."

I stole a look at my sandwich and Bud Light. At least I was saving a few calories on the beer.

"Keep munching like that, and I'll have to call the paramedics to lift you off the sofa."

Sometimes I found Kate quite funny when she was angry. She waited for my reaction, but I refused to give her the satisfaction.

"And since when do you drink beer?"

I picked up the bottle. "Oh, this? I guess I got hooked on those beer commercials. One thing led to another."

She shook her head. "And don't you think you ought to get dressed? It's the afternoon for God's sake!"

I clicked good-bye to Giada and scratched my three-day growth. "I'm tired. Maybe I'm coming down with something."

Kate scowled. "You complained about that yesterday and the day before that. Admit it, Eddie, you're bored and you look like crap. I told you structure is important in retirement. You're going to wind up like Jeff Orenstein."

I shook my head. "Who the hell is he?"

"He's the husband of my cousin Jenny's best friend's friend Denise."

I closed my eyes to detangle the puzzle. "You gotta help me here, Kate. Who?"

"You met him at Jenny's wedding."

I did a quick calculation. "Hasn't she been married over twenty-five years?" I grabbed the neck of the bottle and took a slug.

"Yes, but we had this conversation recently."

"About Jenny?"

"Denise. You're not listening."

I waved the remote. "I give up. What about the guy?"

"He couldn't find himself in retirement and had a nervous breakdown. Poor Jeff had to be hospitalized."

I sat up straight. "No kidding, that Jeff?"

Kate wagged her finger. "Don't mock me, Eddie, I'm trying to make a point here."

"Me too," I said, ripping a god-awful burp with the last gulp of my beer. "Why are you telling me about some guy I have nothing in common with?"

"That's the point, Eddie: You don't get it."

I folded back into the sofa and stared at the empty bottle.

"You remind me of your stepfather," she said with a look of disgust. "Lying around all day on the sofa, drinking beer, and watching that stupid tube. The only thing missing is the ball cap."

"I can wear mine if you like," I said. Oops, that wasn't good.

"Go head, Eddie, mock me again, but if you think I'm just going to put up with this bullshit, you're mistaken."

"What does that mean?"

"You'll see." She stormed out.

I crossed the room for another cold brew, then plopped back on the sofa, flipped the remote, and ran through the channels. Giving up, I tossed aside the remote and glanced at a family photo on the end table. It had been taken soon after my stepfather retired, and he was smiling. I struggled off the couch, picked up the photo, and saluted him with my Bud. Welcome to retirement, Eddie.

Max smiled back. "Your mother drove me crazy too," he had told me on many occasions.

"I remember."

"But I was happy anyway. We both were, even though your mother was always chewing me out about something."

"Like when you wore your Yankee cap throughout the entire Masters Series," I said. "It drove her crazy."

"I don't remember that, Eddie."

"Come on, Max. She argued that hats were meant to be worn outdoors."

"Oh, right. What a ball breaker . . . me, I mean. Your mother was a saint."

I smiled. "Maybe not a saint, but a good woman."

"And a great golfer with a terrific swing."

"Yeah, for a seventy-year-old. You had a pretty good drive yourself, as I recall Mom telling me."

"Until I broke my hip trying to swing like a twenty-year-old."

I sighed. "You found your way, Max, even after golf."

"Here's the thing, Eddie. We all find our way. Some people just take longer than others. You'll find it too. You have to give it time and stop comparing generations. Don't analyze retirement to the nth degree like you were an accountant.'

"I am an accountant."

"Right. Just enjoy one day at a time. You'll see."

"I don't know, Max. I feel like I already lost my way. Actually, I never had a real plan to begin with."

"Maybe you should talk to someone about your situation. How about Jesse? He's a great therapist; I used him myself. You remember, I was a little lost for a while, and I wasn't of the generation who went to therapy. But Jesse picked up on my melancholy, and we had some good talks."

"Gee, Max, I don't know. He's my son, a little too close."

"Close, smosh, he knows about depression."

"Who said anything about being depressed, Max?"

"Max?"

I rubbed my eyes and struggled over to the patio slider to gaze out. I no longer had a view of a canal, pool, or those beautiful white herons. I felt trapped in a twenty-by-twenty walled patio like an inmate with no escape plan.

"What's happening here, Max?"

PERIOD OF ADJUSTMENT

Maybe Max was right. Or whoever it was in my head. I had never been to a shrink, nor taken meds for depression. But lately I'd been drifting into unfamiliar territory, feeling a bit lost.

Of course, those thoughts never surfaced to Kate, but my actions—or rather inactions—evidently were noticeable, as Kate shot her . . . Kate look. Her nagging about structure peaked, but my stubbornness didn't allow me to believe I was that bad off. Maybe I'd been deluding myself that this would pass and that my high spirits would return. As my rudderless days continued, the fog forecast the truth: Eddie Short was entering a storm.

Kate's reaction only reinforced her concern. And helplessness. And Kate never showed helplessness. She didn't push the Jeff Orenstein button, for which I was grateful because, quite frankly, I didn't want to be compared to some guy who lost it. But I had gained more than fifteen pounds since retirement and was fighting with my slacks—on the rare occasions I wore them. I hardly ventured out except to my cellblock patio to water the plants.

I knew Kate was discussing the situation with Jesse, who was calling me more frequently, even during his business hours. We'd chat, or rather he'd do most of the talking, which was unusual for a shrink. They usually listened. But my son knew me too well, so there was no need to probe my past for skeletons. Apparently, I wasn't the best patient, so Jesse decided to pay me a visit. Not wanting any part of my therapy session, Kate took off for the mall, not that she needed an incentive.

For the occasion, I shaved my three-day stubble and found a new "I Love New York" T-shirt I bought in New York City's Chinatown a year ago that didn't need washing. I wasn't so sure about the shorts, though.

All smiles, we faced off sitting in the living room. Jesse also was dressed in shorts and an "I Love New York" T-shirt—I had bought two that year.

"So, Eddie, what don't you like about yourself?"

We shared a laugh to dissolve the ice. It was the opening line from the Nip/Tuck cable series about two Miami Beach plastic surgeons that Jesse and I used to discuss after each episode.

"Everything, these days," I finally said deadpan.

Jesse nodded sympathetically, waiting for me to continue. I was comfortable entering Jesse's psychological world vicariously, though we rarely talked about me unless it included Kate. So I tried circumventing the meat of his inquiry by saying, "I think my serotonin level is depleted."

He nodded again, threading his fingers. "Could be, dad. Lack of serotonin certainly contributes to depression."

"I'm not depressed. It's a chemical imbalance. I probably just need a boost of vitamin B12."

Jesse laughed. "Did you surf the Net for answers, or have you spoken to your doctor about this?"

I shrugged. "A bunch of interesting health sites. Anyway, I figured I'd hold off seeing my doctor, just in case my energy returns."

Jesse didn't pussyfoot around. He said I probably wouldn't improve unless I dug for the root of the problem.

"What am I, a vegetable?" I said.

Jesse ignored my humor and urged me to talk to someone about my funk.

"You mean, like see a shrink?" I forced a smile. "Jesse, that's what I have you for."

He smiled. "You always have me, Dad, but you might want to consider a third party."

I gazed beyond Jesse through the sliding doors. "I don't know if I can do that, son, talk to a complete stranger."

Jesse rolled his eyes. "Dad, your life is an open book. You talk to strangers all the time."

"Yeah, but not about … this."

"This is important. Talking to a psychologist can be a very therapeutic experience. I went through the process myself during the graduate program. It works." He leaned in closer. "First, you build up trust with your therapist to get to the root of the problem. Then you work from there. . . . Dad, you're not the first person to be confused about retirement. It's unfamiliar territory to most people. Look, you worked at the same place for thirty-something years. You had a structured life. Now all of a sudden, you have neither. Sure, the beginning is liberating. No one to tell you what to do …"

"Except your mother," I interrupted.

He laughed. "Right, but then it's just you wondering what to do for the next twenty years. It can be daunting."

My kid obviously knew his stuff. I was feeling better by the minute. "Couldn't I just see my family doctor, get a serotonin boost, and see what happens?"

"The silver bullet therapy." He laughed.

"Something like that. Look, Jesse, you know me as well as anyone outside your mother. I never get depressed. This is situational."

He gave me that look of enough research already, but he did agree it probably was situational. "I'm only suggesting therapy. If you're asking me if I have a problem with you taking antidepressants, I don't."

I leaned in closer as though Kate were in the next room. "Here's the thing. Your mother can keep herself busy talking to herself, but I need to be around people. Ever since we moved here, our social life has died. We haven't made new friends, which is okay with your mother." I paused to make a point. "I need more."

"You feel empty without your friends."

I smiled wistfully. "Very. It's not like I want to go back to work, but I miss the water cooler days, the schmoozing, and the interaction with the guys."

"What I'm hearing is that retirement took away your social lifeline."

"Exactly. See, you understand me better than any therapist."

"You mean any other therapist," he said, smiling.

I returned his smile. "Most of my friends still work, and the few who don't are busy doing other things, or live too far to visit. . . . It's not like your mother and I don't get along. We do. But I still need my guy friends. Does that sound corny?"

He shook his head slowly. "Not at all. It's obvious you need to connect with them, possibly meet after work, play cards, or go to movies. Stuff like that."

"I thought about it, Jesse, but it's a bit of a trip back to the old neighborhood."

He laughed. "I remember you telling me it was only an hour away."

"Poor night vision," I began, then stopped.

Jesse admonished me, insisting excuses were easier than commitments, and if I really wanted to see my friends, I'd find a way. Then he offered suggestion. "You might consider doing some volunteer work. That's a great way to meet people. Do tax returns for people at your community center."

I frowned. "I hate taxes."

Jesse shrugged. "It doesn't have to be taxes. Any volunteer work will keep you engaged."

I nodded. "I'll keep that in mind." The thought didn't excite me, though.

Jesse shook his head and smiled.

"What?"

"Join a fly-fishing club? You bought the equipment."

I laughed. "I'm thinking of selling it on eBay."

Jesse leaned back in his chair and crossed his legs. "Thinking too far ahead can be intimidating, Dad. Consider doing something over the next year or even the next six months. But you need to stop sitting around feeling sorry for yourself."

I was about to protest but stopped. "I am, aren't I?"

Jesse didn't answer. He didn't have to.

I felt better after talking. As Jesse departed, he gave me a hug and kissed my forehead. "You'll be fine, Dad."

"No nervous breakdown?" I asked tenuously.

He shook his head. "Though you might give Mom one if you don't shape up."

"We don't need two neurotic people in the family." I chuckled.

"You're going through a crisis that will take some work. You up for it?"

I shrugged. "I'll give it a try."

Jesse turned to leave, then stopped. "And remember me when you guys need an extra poker player. I could use the money."

THE ART OF COOKING

You're only as good as your last dose of meds.

I had felt great since my doctor prescribed Celexa 20 mg. At first, I nearly panicked. Possible side effects included mood or behavioral changes, anxiety, panic attacks, trouble sleeping, feeling impulsive, irritable, agitated, hostile, aggressive, restless, hyperactive, more depressed, or even suicidal thoughts. Good God, I kept waiting for my first panic attack—to attack! But after a week, the meds kicked in, and now I was the old me again. I wasn't looking to run for poster child, but my energy level and mental health had spiked tenfold. Plus, a sense of calmness had settled in that I hadn't noticed before. I felt more focused.

Yet strangely, I felt I was cheating, passing the grade without taking a test. Perhaps that's what Jesse alluded to when he recommended therapy in conjunction with the antidepressants:

getting to the root of my problem while feeling comfortable and capable of addressing the issues. I couldn't say whether I'd incorporate therapy because the silver bullet seemed to be working just fine for now. In any event, my family doctor recommended we revisit my condition in about a year.

My home life couldn't have been better either. I became more involved with Kate, even driving her around and helping her pick out color schemes for the house. She didn't appear to mind, and quite frankly, respected my suggestions. I never thought I had a flair for decorating, but I was excited again. About life! My serotonin level must have been depleted since birth.

After a few hours of ambling about at the mall with Kate one day, I noticed her taking shorter strides, not jabbering about fabrics. She wanted to go home to take a nap.

"You sure?" I asked. "Because I'm good."

She dropped down on a wooden bench and looked up at me. "You're not tired?"

I shrugged. "Me? Nope. Bring on more color schemes."

Kate narrowed her eyes. "I ought to consider taking what you're on."

"What?"

"The meds, Eddie. How could you forget?" Kate bent down and massaged her ankles. "You've been forgetting a lot lately. Must be a side effect."

"Beats me." I sat down beside her. "All I know is those nasty early side effects disappeared. It's scary not being able to get it up."

Kate scowled. "Eddie, be discreet."

I glanced at two elderly women passing by. "Sorry."

She yawned. "Let's go home. And I'm not cooking tonight, so we're stuck with your culinary skills. Any ideas, Mr. Chef?"

"Me? Let me think about it." I didn't, of course, and I felt the pressure of a freight train while driving home. As we passed a shopping plaza, I motioned to a Chinese restaurant. "How about takeout?"

Kate, leaning back in her seat with her eyes closed, laughed to herself. "Apparently, serotonin doesn't boost cooking levels, I see."

I waited for her to approve the Chinese, but she wasn't in the mood. I watched the plaza fade in my rearview mirror. "Weren't you the one who said I couldn't boil water?" I asked, trying to evade a potential disaster.

Kate turned her head an inch toward me and opened an eye. "I simply implied that when you boil water for tea, the tea bag should, at some point, be placed in the cup. Tea just doesn't appear."

"You also told me a salad is more than just tearing off a head of lettuce."

"And you proved me right. That's why it's time you started taking charge of the kitchen occasionally. Think about the future. What would you do if I wasn't around to cook anymore?"

I twisted my lips. "You mean like taking a trip by yourself for a week?"

"What if I got sick?" Both eyes opened.

"Oh, I'd call out for something."

"Worse than just sick."

I loved teasing Kate. She was avoiding dead. "I'm not following. What could happen?"

"Oh, for God's sake, Eddie. If I had a dreaded disease or died."

"Which one?"

Kate huffed. "You're impossible."

"I get your point, Kate. I'd call out for Chinese."

"Every day?"

"Heck no. I have a file on all the restaurants in the area. There's Vinny's—"

"Eddie!"

I turned my head slightly. "You're not preparing me for something, are you, Kate?"

"I'm fine, Eddie, though you drive me nuts sometimes. Call out for Chinese when I'm dead!"

I brushed her hand. "Come on, I get your point."

She waited a moment. "Now that you're out of your funk, you need to channel some of your energy into more productive activities. Tonight's dinner is a start."

I stared at the road. "Like when I was working?"

"Eddie, you were never working. You were employed."

"A technicality. Okay, what's your poison tonight?"

Kate closed her eyes and leaned back on the headrest. "Anything but Chinese."

Back at home, the kitchen felt like a foreign country. "How about a little cooking workshop before I begin?" I asked.

Kate rolled her eyes and bent down to look in a cabinet drawer. I watched her wiggle and fantasized of how I could get around cooking. When Kate found a cookbook, she turned and caught my elfish smile.

"Don't even think about it, Eddie. Sex is your avoidance to anything productive. I'm hungry and you're cooking. And if you don't learn to cook something edible, you might become celibate." She handed me Cookbook for Dummies. "Pick something easy. . . . Oh, what was I thinking?"

After she abandoned me for the sofa, I skimmed my finger down and up the index page—and down again. This was going to be tough. I stopped at a familiar recipe. "Found one."

"It better not be that cheesy meatloaf!" she called out. "That was a disaster last time you attempted it. We almost had to call the paramedics."

I nodded. For sure. I continued and stopped at my next favorite.

"And don't even consider the tuna casserole. Last time you drowned it in water."

Scratch two. There had to be some easy dish I could make, but it appeared I was in trouble.

Kate must have noticed my silence. "OK, champ, pick one already, and I'll hold your hand for a while. I'm famished."

My eyes stopped at the baked macaroni and cheese, and I told Kate it would take twenty minutes tops.

Kate rolled off the sofa and grabbed the holy book from my hand. "Let me see that. . . . You didn't read the fine print. It's twenty to prepare and twenty to bake. That means you can't stay on the Internet very long. Knowing how lost you get online, I recommend setting the timer. You know where the timer is, don't you, Eddie?"

I walked over to the microwave and pressed start.

Kate shook her head. "Close." She pressed stop. "It's the button underneath." She pointed at a cabinet. "How about getting the ingredients in the drawer? I'll wait."

I read the recipe and searched for the black pepper. "Where do you keep the pepper?" I asked innocently.

"How long—? Never mind." Kate grabbed the pepper and placed it on the counter. "Really, what would you do if I were dead?"

"Get married—quickly!"

"You're probably better off ordering Chinese. You men don't know how to fend for yourselves. I guess that's why you keep getting married. What's next on your list?"

"Bread crumbs."

"And?"

"After the bread crumbs?"

"No, Eddie, where are the bread crumbs?"

"Trick question?"

She sighed. "We should have done takeout." She removed the bread crumbs from another drawer. And in seconds, she lined the remaining ingredients up like wooden soldiers. "Go for it."

I followed the instructions, satisfied.

"What do you think?" I turned, but Kate had disappeared. I shrugged, placed the casserole dish in the oven, and turned on the timer before sneaking into my cave to check my e-mail.

Like clockwork, the timer chirped in twenty minutes. "Time to feed that empty stomach!" I called out with pride.

"In a minute."

I turned off the timer and opened the oven door like an accomplished chef. "Shit," I said a little too loud.

"The oven has to be turned on, Eddie. Twenty minutes at 400 degrees!" Kate called out.

How'd she know?

GOLF FORE ME?

I wasn't a jock. Outside of little league baseball, I rarely played sports. Even as a spectator, I didn't venture beyond the World Series or Super Bowl, so Kate didn't suffer from football widow syndrome. Internet syndrome was another story, though.

During my high school days, the Marist brothers—a Catholic congregation of religious teaching brothers—forced us into an annual track and field event. I protested to my homeroom teacher, Mr. Neumann, a lay teacher. (I always wondered what that term meant, considering it was a boys school.) Anyway, Mr. Neumann assured me it was a day off from studies and "a walk in the park." Easy for him to say, considering he wasn't required to "walk in the park." Mr. Neumann said the brothers were serious about physical exercise, and no student other than the physically challenged would be excused. He locked eyes with me as he emphasized physically, not mentally. Then he cracked up, leaving me feeling physically and mentally neutered.

My community college accepted any high school diploma, so I was about to become the first member of my dysfunctional family to graduate—if I could pass a phys-ed elective. I eliminated football because of my lightweight size, baseball for lack of speed, and track for lack of interest. Down to tennis and bowling. Golf wasn't an elective in my school, which I would have considered if it came with a cart. I was a gutter ball guy when bowling, so I opted for tennis. I bought a second-hand racket from a friend who aced the class. I hoped it symbolized good luck.

Wrong! Tennis was a game of concentration, stamina, and above all, power. A Wild West home life had shot my concentration years before. But even under the best of circumstances, how could a student concentrate when our instructor, an idiot from some upstate New York college, hadn't bothered to size us up according to height, weight, or gender? You'd think he would have encouraged us to learn the sport. After giving us a few elementary instructions, he hauled our asses onto the courts with no plan, mismatching everyone, which, if you could visualize, created a more circus effect than a Hollywood choreographic set. Imagine a six-foot jock slamming a yellow hairy ball at a mousy four-foot-eight woman—with glasses, no less. I swore his intention was to ruin her ability to conceive.

Then there was the stamina problem. Try running around a court when you started smoking at thirteen. My only hope was power. Nail it on the first serve. That was easier if you were six foot, but I was a mere five-five in college. (I grew to a whopping five-six, thanks to my father's genes). He was reduced to buying size 5 shoes from Buster Brown for kids.

In humiliating fashion, I lost every set to a six-foot Amazon named Mary Jo, who should have been exempt from phys-ed. After the final match with Miss Iron Hand, I trudged to my instructor's office, where he was giving a private golf lesson to a young, sexy woman who had to stretch her arms around her enormous breasts to putt. He scowled at me.

"Is there a possibility I can be matched with an opponent who is not so professional?" I asked, watching his huge jock hands inch up the student's arm toward her double D cups.

"Who's your opponent?" His hands stopped at her elbows.

"Mary Jo something or other. She's nice, but I can't manage to lob the ball back to her."

He stepped back and rubbed his chin. "Sorry, did you say Mary Jo?"

I panicked. Did he have some special interest in her? I nodded sheepishly.

"That's a girl, right?"

My expression changed to confusion. "A very big girl . . . with more experience than the class put together."

He turned to the student, then back to me. “Still, she’s a girl. What’s your name?”

“Eddie Short, coach.”

“I’m not your coach, Eddie, I’m your instructor. Anyway, I did you a favor. The only way to learn is to play against a better player.”

“But …”

He raised his hand. “Relax, Eddie, grades aren’t based on the number of games you win, but on how much you improve throughout the course.” He smiled. “Know what I mean?”

“Really?” Maybe I actually had a shot at passing.

“Sure. Otherwise, half of the class would fail.”

I stole a peek at Miss DD still in her putting stance. “Makes sense, I guess.”

His eyes softened as he approached me. “Nobody fails my class, not even you. Now go back and give Mary Jo something or other a run for her money.”

I nodded. “Thanks for the encouragement, coach.”

“No problem. And if you’re interested in golf, I give private lessons, reasonable rates for my students.” He turned back to his current specimen who had an A written all over her face.

“I’ll keep that in mind,” I said, heading for the door. And fuck you!

Even though Kate knew I was sports challenged, she surprised me with a set of golf clubs, a golf bag, shoes, and a funny outfit. The whole thing smelled like a setup.

"I don't know what to say, dear," I said, kissing her on the cheek.

Kate took in a lungful of air. "Now that we finished decorating the house, you have more time on your hands."

Translation: Kate wanted me out of the house. I pulled a club out of the bag and took a short swing, feigning confidence. "It's light."

"It's graphite," she said with authority. "The salesman called it a hybrid. He said it takes the place of a three and four iron."

I nodded, impressed with Kate's sudden knowledge, and replaced the club with the putter. "Sounds like you did your homework."

"The guy at the sporting goods store gave me a quick lesson." She smiled encouragingly.

I drew back the club straight like I'd seen Tiger do. "I think I can get into this."

"Told you." She sounded relieved. "It's a great sport for you, Eddie, not too strenuous. And you get exercise."

Right. "Wanna join me?" I asked innocently, meeting her eyes.

Kate shook her head with a look of panic. "Gee, Eddie, I don't think golf is for me. Besides, I'm thinking of branching out with my interior designing."

"Branching out?" I snickered. "Too bad. We could play as a couple."

"We already spend a lot of time together—meals, movies, the theater."

I nodded. "I suppose. It's just that I have to find three people to play with. You need a foursome in golf. Did the sales guy tell you that?"

Kate smiled widely. "He said it shouldn't be a problem. Just show up at the course. People are always looking for a fourth."

I nodded again, not convinced. "Yeah, but I hate being a fifth wheel."

"You won't be. You'll be a fourth wheel." She laughed nervously. "Come on, Eddie, give it a try. You'll meet people this way."

I rubbed my chin. "Maybe you're right. I could use a few friends."

Kate handed me an envelope from her back pocket. "Here's the best part. Open it."

It was a certificate for golf lessons. Wow!

"You might even make new friends at the clinic," she said, pushing.

"Gee, Kate, I don't know what to say. Thanks." I kissed her passionately.

"I love guys with graphite clubs." She moaned. "How about you start your lessons right here, Mr. Golfman?"

That was the beauty of retirement: always time for sex. It was early afternoon, not a care in the world, and my wife was not of childbearing age. Yeah, I had been had, but hey, the sex was good.

PLEASE DON'T FAIL ME!

The golf clinic was located at the public golf course a few minutes from my house. I arrived early for my first lesson and took a seat. Within minutes, a few guys my age entered the cavernous room with similar golf bags and outfits. Sports Authority must have run an ad last weekend saying "Special for wives trying to engage their husbands in outdoor activities." Our wives wouldn't be sending us prowling around if we were twenty years younger.

I pointed at my neighbor's bag as he sat down with more hair than Samson. "First time?"

He nodded. "The wife wants me out of the house. You?"

"She's hoping I'll be the next geriatric Tiger Woods so I can buy her a Mercedes."

He laughed. "My wife already has a Mercedes. She's looking for me to get out of her hair."

Bragger. "Retired?"

"Six months ago. I took an early out from the power company."

"Good deal, I'm guessing."

He smiled. "A deal I couldn't resist. Otherwise, I would have had to hang around another five years. Unfortunately, most of my friends are stuck in miserable jobs and can't retire because they're not sixty-five and can't afford medical insurance. You?"

"Federal pension with health insurance. I was ready to go."

He thought a moment. "Your wife okay with it? You know, being home all the time?"

I nosed my golf bag. "She's hoping I'll get in thirty-six holes a day."

He laughed. "They must have been watching the same talk show."

"Sure looks that way." I extended my hand. "I'm Eddie."

"Joe," he said, shaking mine.

"Maybe after our lessons, if we're still interested, we can play a round together."

"Sure, but you do know we'll need two more for a foursome? It's in the bylaws or something."

"Right." The two other guys in the room apparently were listening to our conversation. "Say, would you guys be interested in a foursome?" Um, that didn't come out right, but they accepted.

"We're new to the game," one of them said.

"Great." I was getting excited about my new golf buddies.

The door opened, and a tall guy with a shiny pate stuck his head in. "If you guys are waiting for lessons, raise your hand."

What, like in school?

We raised our hands in unison.

"Come on in, boys." He smiled.

We pulled our equipment into another room, and the instructor introduced himself. I couldn't help but stare at him. He must have noticed because he asked, "Something wrong?"

I shook my head, but I was struck with panic as I searched the room for an Amazon woman named Mary Jo. Slow down, Eddie, you're not back in tennis class. I tried to settle down and listen to my new/old instructor, Mr. Pissface, who barely passed me thirty-something years ago. Miss Mary Jo got an A, as did every woman in his class, the prick.

So, after all those years, I shuddered at the thought that he might fail me. To my surprise, it went smoothly. Then again, there weren't any women to distract Mr. Put Out For Me For An A. I learned a few swing techniques and began feeling comfortable with my clubs. Of course, that was before we starting hitting balls.

The second lesson was held at the range where our instructor kept us away from the other golfers so we wouldn't distract them—though I didn't consider myself a golfer yet.

Mr. Pissface motioned to me. "How about you go first, Eddie? Place the ball on the rubber tee, address the ball, and swing. Take your time and follow through like I showed you in class."

I nodded, followed his instruction, and took a full swing when I worked up enough courage. My eyes followed what I imagined the ball's trajectory would be. Then I looked down and swore. Please don't fail me at my age, not in front of my new friends.

"It's kind of like the first time you have sex, Eddie," Mr. Pissface said with a philosophical air. "If you try too hard, nothing happens."

Great, now I was getting a sex lesson!

"Try again. This time, take a deep breath and follow the ball like I showed you. Remember, it's not a baseball bat, so you don't have to swing hard. The wrist will take care of the ball."

I addressed the ball again, took a few moments to collect myself, and swung. I heard a snap, thank God, and smiled with satisfaction.

"Nice shot!" the guys cried out and giggled. I gazed out but spotted my ball smiling back at me a few feet away.

Mr. Pissface rested his hand on my shoulder. "Don't worry about the distance; you hit the ball." And with that, the group clapped. What a game.

The rest of the guys followed my road to stardom, and I was relieved I wasn't the worst.

At the end of our final lesson, I waited for the others to leave before approaching my former instructor. I asked him if he recognized me.

He shook his head. "From where?"

"Think tennis."

He cocked his head as though for divine intervention and squinted back at me. "I used to teach tennis at Queensborough Community College in New York, but that was years ago. You attend that school?"

I nodded. "When I had more hair."

"Me too." He laughed and patted his stomach. "I was twenty pounds lighter. You weren't in any of my classes, were you?"

"Oh yeah, think Amazon."

"Amazon? I'm afraid I don't understand."

I refreshed his memory about the way he matched the students in a very uneven order, pairing me up with Mary Jo, the Amazon. "I will say this about Mary Jo; I wanted to make passionate love with her. As I remember, she had great tits!"

His face turned cold. "Mary Jo was my wife."

I swallowed hard. "Oh, she had a hell of a backhand."

His eyes narrowed. "Now I remember you. You were that wimpy guy who complained about her. God, you were pathetic. A girl whipping your ass."

Hostility etched his face. Fortunately, I had taken an assertiveness course at work. I locked eyes. "She probably kicked your ass too."

He squeezed the three-iron in his hand as though it were my neck. Apparently, the course hadn't taught us how to deal with lunatics. I didn't want Kate's gift to be wasted before my first game, so I said in a conciliatory tone, "Anyway, that was the past."

But his expression didn't change. "She died asshole. And for your information she was a great athlete." He tossed the three-iron to the side and bolted for the parking lot.

"Hey, Coach! For what it's worth, I was a pussy back then."

BROTHER, CAN YOU SPARE A JOB?

Out of curiosity, my fingers started gravitating toward the jobs classified section of the *Palm Beach Post*. I was psyched about my impending golf match, but really more for the camaraderie than the game itself. Quite frankly, I couldn't see myself wildly swinging a wedge in sand traps or agonizing over lost balls all the time.

Unfortunately, I mentioned my concerns to Kate, who recited her usual spiel about me squandering my time. "There's more to life than sitting around playing on the Internet, Eddie." Foolish me.

I admitted Kate's perception of my life was accurate. To think otherwise would be delusional. And while I initially enjoyed my life of nothingness, the easy life as Kate called it, I was beginning to think life was too easy. Hence, my interest in the employment section.

Plenty of jobs were waiting for warm bodies, though most I had no business entertaining. Take nightclub jobs, for example. Bartenders–I didn't know a thing about pouring drinks. Cocktail servers—I never looked good in corsets or tights. Dancers . . . I noticed an ad for a timeshare salesperson, but I gave up selling snake oil years ago.

There were positions for guys good with their hands. I knew a few who started at Home Depot and Lowe's after retirement. I wasn't handy and couldn't tell the difference between a wrench and pliers, though I think Kate complemented me once after screwing in a light bulb. Got lucky, I guessed.

Sales positions were abundant, but salaries generally were based on commissions or slightly higher than minimum wage, so I dismissed those. Actually, there was another reason: Even though I was friendly, I wouldn't enjoy dealing with customers who returned broken items or dresses worn once, usually after a special occasion. I was a taxman my entire adult life. Giving a refund was not in my mission statement. And while job titles such as sales associate, inside sales, or account executive sounded interesting, they were meant for young, hungry whippersnappers. I wasn't hungry nor interested in a high-pressure job. "Cooking" on occasion was about all I could handle.

Companies also were looking for accountants and bookkeepers or other financial types. Perhaps I could work for a tax company such as H&R Block, but in reality, if I never saw another tax return again, including mine, I'd die a happy man. As Leona Helmsley used to say, "Only little people pay taxes." I would never sign off on tax returns for little people who claimed their pets.

Eventually, I came across a guardhouse job at a gated community. If I wasn't interested in living in a gated community, why would I want to guard one? Quite honestly, I wanted a part-time job where I could fall out of bed and begin the day. Kate would suggest cleaning the house.

I finally shared my job prospects with Kate, whose enthusiasm was self-serving, so I decided to throw out the question to Jesse one evening after dinner.

"I think it's a great idea, Dad. It will give you and Mom a break from each other." He picked up on my frown and backed off his comment. That was my son, the diplomat. Actually, Kate and I hadn't been bumping into each other as often, probably because she managed to find projects far away from my cave.

"I've been searching the help-wanted ads, but can't find anything suitable." I shrugged. "And I don't want to prepare tax returns."

Jesse mulled my response. "Instead of seeking employment, how about going back to school to start a second career? It'll give your brain a great workout."

"School? As in study and tests?"

"Why not?" His eyes lit up at the remote thought I'd take him up on it.

"My brain died years ago. Besides, I don't think I could sit still for more than a few minutes."

"You'd feel young again around students."

I waved him off. "They'll be calling me grandpa, Jesse. I'd be embarrassed."

Jesse waited a moment. "How about an online course?"

"Computer class?"

"Work at your own pace, get up for coffee when you wanted—"

"Or pee when I had to. That might work. But I wasn't thinking of a second career, Jesse. I only want to get out of the house for a few hours."

He nodded. "How about a Realtor?"

I shook my head. "The market is down the tubes now."

Jesse rubbed his chin and smiled. "You have any phobias, Dad?"

I stared at him. "Phobias?"

"You know, like shaking hands."

I never thought about it. "Don't believe so."

His smile widened. "How about a greeter?"

I laughed hysterically. "You're good. You almost had me for a minute."

He didn't share my levity.

"What, you mean like, 'Hi, I'm Eddie, welcome to Walmart?' "

He remained silent to let it sink in. I certainly was capable of smiling and shaking hands with customers, but only old guys did that. I reminded my son I was a bit of a snob since his mother dragged me to stores such as Bloomingdale's and Nordstrom. "As far as I know, they don't hire greeters."

Jesse shrugged. "Sorry, Dad, I'm out of ideas."

After Jesse left, I turned on the tube and caught a commercial with someone in a chicken outfit flapping their wings wildly in front of a Chicken Moma fast-food restaurant as drivers honked their horns. A real celebrity.

That was it! I could work incognito, didn't have to smile, and the costume would protect me if I had to shake hands. The next day, I called the franchise in my neighborhood to ask if they had an opening. My excitement must have made an impression on the guy.

"You're not some kind of pervert, are you?" he asked.

"What?"

"Well, you seem too excited for a job that pays minimum wage. There are no free chicken lunches either, and you're not entitled to discounts for the first three months. You still interested?"

I told him I resented the accusation and he could check with the police. And as for free chicken lunches, my wife made great peanut butter-and-jelly sandwiches.

"That sounds like a yes. Nothing personal, buddy, but sometimes we have to ask because some of our business caters to kids' birthdays and such, so we have to be careful who we hire."

"Well, I'm certainly not into kids that way," I said testily.

"Sorry if I offended you, but we've had problems in the past. You sound more normal now that you've calmed down."

"I assure you I'm very normal."

"Great, when can you come in for an interview?"

"I'm available anytime."

"So you don't work then?"

"I'm retired."

"That's even better. Older folks tend to work better and stay longer than college students looking for a quick buck."

I wanted to respond that minimum wage was less than a quick buck, but I already had a strike against me. The next day, I arrived and found the six-foot Chicken Moma mascot outside shaking his hands wildly.

"Hey, buddy!" he cried out, approaching me. "Welcome to Chicken Moma where great food and service are second to none."

I shook his white-gloved hand. "Nice grip."

"You should have seen me forty years ago when I played varsity."

"I can imagine. Say, is it really hot in there?"

"In here where I am or in the store?" He laughed. "It's okay right now, but the summers are brutal. That's when I head to the mountains."

"Smart. So you'll be working here for a while?"

"Hope so, I need the money." He laughed again. "Actually, I'm the owner's dad. As soon as he finds a replacement, I'm out of here. Need a job? I got connections." He snickered through his costume.

A sense of humor probably was helpful inside that outfit all day.

"I'm thinking about it, actually. But let me ask you another question: How do you do it? You know, pee? I don't see a fly."

"Oh, that." He glanced around before stepping closer. "Depends."

"On what?"

"Depends, Pampers, you know, I pee in here."

My face turned to horror. "You can't be serious."

He cracked up and rubbed my head. "Just kidding, buddy. It takes a little longer, but hey, I'm not on a schedule." He extended his hand again. "I'm Bill. You must be the new guy."

"How did you guess?" I asked, shaking his hand.

"You ask a lot of questions. Besides, my son mentioned someone was showing up."

"Oh."

"I was a New York City detective for twenty years, so I can smell when someone is up to something. Not that you were up to anything bad. Anyway, Junior is expecting you."

I glanced inside. "Thanks."

"And remember the summers."

I watched Bill move back to his work zone next to passing cars. Not too close to the curb, Bill.

NEW FRIENDS

Moving into a retirement community and meeting people fifty-five plus could be challenging. Unless you frequented bars for the old set, nude beaches for retirees, or doctors' offices, the last being the easiest. But was I desperate enough to listen to poor-me medical problems all day? Hell, I might as well volunteer at a hospital.

People in retirement communities had at least one thing in common: age, obviously. But that circled back to endless medical discussions in those fancy clubhouses. Another drawback: The average age generally was fifty-five plus twenty, so friends were hard to keep, considering the U.S. mortality rate was around seventy-seven for men and eighty-one for women. The upshot for me, of course, was the opportunity to replace the passed souls with younger blood . . . until my ticket on the mortality radar grew close at hand.

Many of my friends in Broward County swore by those retirement communities and the more isolated I became, the more I wondered if they were on to something. I was banking on my golf buddies staying healthy and filling the void, if only once a week.

We scheduled our first round of golf the day we completed the class. Professor Pissface didn't fail anyone. I had almost a week to tee-day and got a head start by hitting a few balls at the range. Frustration set in almost immediately, but I vowed to continue. I also swore off cheating unless my ball landed too close to a tree, or got lost, but only if my partners weren't watching.

When I arrived for our first blowout, two of our foursome were signing us in, so I ventured down to the practice area to putt. Soon after, the guys joined me. Carl, a six-footer with a flock of gray hair, towered over his younger cousin, Henry, who sported a new dark-brown hair piece that matched his outfit. They moved to South Florida a few year back after selling their frozen food business in Minnesota. That sounded like an oxymoron.

"Joe isn't here yet," Carl said. "At least he hasn't signed in."

Joe Ricardo, our fourth, was a transplant Jersey guy who, like me, retired early.

"Anyone hear from him?" I asked, checking my watch.

The cousins shook their heads.

"I hope he shows. This is our first outing." I absently putted a ball and missed the hole by a few feet.

"The starter said we'll have to be assigned a fourth," Carl said with a shrug. "In case Joe doesn't show up."

I nodded. Did this have to do with health issues, a doctor's appointment perhaps? Or, maybe he just forgot. In that case, Joe might have a different health issue.

I grabbed my balls—off the ground—and followed the Minnesotans to the first tee where the starter, a retirement type in shorts, was chatting with a woman around minimum drinking age. His T-shirt read, "I'm spending my children's inheritance."

He waved us over. "Your fourth show up yet?"

I shook my head.

He smiled, motioning to the young woman. "Well, today's your lucky day, fellows. This is Julie Ann. I know her family, so go easy on her." He suppressed a laugh.

My eyes brightened. At least I had something more interesting to watch besides dribbling balls.

Carl and Henry acted like they were in heat. Just shameful. She smiled and shook their hands. She then smiled at me, which I returned like a schoolboy. Shameful.

Julie Ann, a student at Auburn University, was visiting her family for a few days. Lucky us. Sorry, Joe.

"Do you come here often?" Carl asked, sounding like the sixties.

Her long blonde hair was pulled tight in a ponytail. "Play here? Occasionally when I'm home from school. My dad and I usually get in a round when he's not working. You guys?"

I snickered. "We're kind of new to the game. I hope we won't drag you down."

She smiled. "Don't worry, sir, my father isn't that great of a player either."

Sir? A formal gal, this Julie Ann. "Great, less pressure."

By the third hole, I was getting into the swing, slicing more, but dribbling less, missing the ball off the tee only twice, which I contributed to Julie Ann's perfume permeating into my tee box. Carl and Henry, on the other hand, lost a half-dozen balls between them. They were more interested in Julie Ann and her swing. She was a natural, her swing flawless, and her putting on the money. She told us her uncle taught her.

"Good shot, sir," she said as my ball sailed about thirty feet down the fairway. On the side, I asked Julie Ann if she wouldn't mind calling me Eddie.

"Sure, sir, I will."

By the ninth hole and almost a dozen balls lost between us guys, we decided to call it a day. I asked Julie Ann if she would mind.

"No, Mister Eddie. I'll be okay."

Mr. Eddie? What an improvement. "Or, if you'd like, you can join us for lunch at the clubhouse."

She glanced up at the ominous sky. “How about a rain check?” She laughed.

“Anytime. Good luck, and thanks for being so patient.”

“I enjoyed playing with you guys . . . Eddie.”

Good girl.

Carl and Henry also took a rain check, so we shook hands and scheduled a game for the following week. “I’ll call Joe and find out what happened,” I said and headed for the clubhouse. Sitting alone, I watched beads of rain hit the window pane before ordering a cheeseburger, fries, and a cold draft. In no time, the window was pelted, and I got worried about Julie Ann.

As though reading my mind, Julie Ann tapped me on the shoulder. “I should have taken you up on lunch.”

I glanced up. “Hey, I was just thinking about you.” Uh, that didn’t sound right. I offered her a cloth napkin for her wet face and beckoned the waitress.

Julie Ann sat down, patted her face, and placed the napkin in her lap. She ordered a Cobb salad and Diet Coke before we launched into small talk about the game.

“So, you like retirement?” she asked.

I hesitated. “Sometimes, I guess, as long as I’m doing something. My wife would agree with that.”

She laughed. “Sounds like you have mixed feelings about leaving the job.”

I pondered her comment. "It wasn't so much the job. I miss the people. Moving away from them didn't help either. We rarely socialize anymore. . . . I'm not quite sure how I fit in with this retirement business, to tell you the truth. I miss not being part of an organization." I shrugged. "I guess I need to reinvent myself."

She nodded, but I doubted a twenty-something could fully understand the hazards of retirement. But it turned out Julie Ann was pursuing a doctorate in psychology and understood plenty.

"You're still young, Eddie. I'm sure you can do anything you like, within reason."

"That's what my son tells me. He's a therapist."

She smiled. "There you go. Some people continue doing what they did during their career."

I nodded. "My son tells me that too. But taxes? I'd rather walk on burning coals."

She laughed. "Maybe you feel that way now, but at some point, you might consider doing it as part of a volunteer program."

"Maybe," I said not enthusiastically.

When our food arrived, I let her taste her salad before saying, "You're a very good player, Julie Ann, and have a terrific swing."

She blushed a little. "Thanks. I must confess it runs in the family. My father is actually a pretty good player."

I smiled. "He must be proud."

"Actually, my first love is swimming."

"Really? Well, actually, that makes sense living in South Florida."

"Except I grew up in South Carolina. We swam mostly indoors. You swim?"

"Only in my bathtub. I'm afraid of the water. I swam into a flounder once at a New York beach. I'll never forgot those eyes."

Julie Ann laughed again. "You're funny, Eddie. I noticed your accent. I have relatives in New York. At least I did. Most of them moved to South Florida."

"That's pretty common. Are they looking for friends?" I was kidding, but it must have sounded terribly desperate in light of our conversation.

"I'm sure they would love to meet you. Give me your phone number." She reached for a sugar packet. "Got a pen?"

I felt silly calling over the waitress to ask for a pen, but I gave Julie Ann my number. The waitress scowled as I returned her pen.

I was about to take a bite of my burger when I caught a familiar face over Julie Ann's shoulder and swore.

"What's wrong?" she asked.

I shook my head. "It's a long story." I nosed beyond her. "My golf instructor, the jerk. He'll probably have something to say about me sitting here with you."

"Really? We're only having lunch."

"Like I said, he's a jerk."

Mr. Jerk caught my stare, and his body stiffened. Julie Ann read my face and turned to see Mr. Jerk. "Uncle Jerry!"

Uncle Jerry? Oh God. Professor Pissface's eyes softened when he spotted Julie Ann and crossed the room.

"I heard you were in town," he said, kissing her cheek while staring me down.

"Eddie, you know my Uncle Jerry, right?" She turned to her uncle. "Eddie is new in the community and is looking for a friend."

Pathetic.

His hostility didn't abate. "Don't you think you're kind of old hitting on young women, especially someone young enough to be your daughter?" He turned to Julie Ann. "I know this guy, he's a jerk."

Julie Ann's face brightened. "That can't be, Uncle Jerry. Eddie was just telling me that he attributed his great swing to his golf instructor."

Pissface eyed me. "That true?"

I nodded amicably. "Absolutely, and what a coincidence that you're related to my golf partner."

Professor Pissface melted into a friendly Uncle Jerry. "You seemed to be a natural."

"Thanks. Want to join us?"

"Gee, I don't know—"

"Oh, please, Uncle Jerry."

He glanced out the window and shrugged. “Sure, why not?” He sat beside his niece who winked at me.

After a few beers, we let our college days die. Uncle Jerry and I became Jerry and Eddie. He told me about his short marriage to Mary Jo, and I nodded in sympathy. My eyes met Julie Ann, and she smiled warmly. The kid was on her way to becoming a great psychologist. I smiled to myself. Two new friends who came with a bonus; Professor Jerry offered me golf lessons at family rates.

FIRST DAY ON THE JOB

I was beginning to fill up my days, so Kate hadn't been poking her head into my cave wondering what the heck I was up to. With a weekly golf outing and working as a Chicken Moma mascot three days a week, I began to sense some stability in my life. Kate supported my mascot job a hundred percent, considering I would be incognito to any embarrassing comments or ridicule.

On the first day of the job, I dressed in a T-shirt, shorts, and sneakers. I didn't bother shaving because my face would be hidden by the costume. Kate waited by the front door like an eager mother sending her kid off to school.

"You look like you're going to the beach, Eddie." She kissed me on the forehead.

"My boss warned that it might get hot inside the costume."

"I guess if it's okay with him." She eyed my face. "You haven't shaved for three days. If I were your boss . . ." She must have assumed I'd become some executive or something.

"He suggested beach casual, whatever that is. And who's going to see me anyway?"

She gave me a "whatever" look. "Are you sure you don't want to take along a sandwich?"

"No, thanks." I smiled. "I persuaded the boss to include a combo meal as part of the deal."

Kate patted me on the head. "That's nice, darling. Don't be late for work."

I opened the door to the Chicken Moma and found Junior waving at me as though relieved I hadn't called in sick. He motioned me over and reached under the counter.

"Hey, Eddie, I got your outfit. I figured you were a medium."

I picked up the costume and stared at its head. "He doesn't look like me. My beak isn't as pronounced."

"Lucky you. The last guy complained it looked too much like him." He laughed. "Anyway, I upgraded the outfit to feet with rubber soles. Dad complained his sneakers showed and didn't look authentic."

"I definitely want to look authentic. Say, is your dad coming in today?"

Junior checked his watch. "He should be here in an hour."

"How will I recognize him? We met when he was in costume."

"He looks like me, only thirty years older with less hair." He laughed again.

A customer walked in as I started putting on the costume, so I moved into the stall and put the beak on the floor. Creepy. Fortunately, it was a one-piece chicken outfit—well two counting the beak—and when I put it on, it felt, well, weird—Halloween weird. Satisfied, I grabbed the beak, pulled it over my head in front of the mirror, and blew myself a kiss.

Armed with coupons and fliers, I walked outside and spread my arms. Oh yeah, a job! The outfit wasn't terribly hot, but it was only ten in the morning. Indiantown Road already was bustling. When passing drivers honked their horns, I got excited and flapped my arms wildly . . . like a chicken. But my arms grew tired, so I stopped waving.

A car slowed down with hazard lights, and I stepped closer to the curb as the tinted passenger window rolled down. I leaned forward to . . . whoa, the kid was mooning me. I recoiled as he ordered a happy meal. At least, it sounded like happy meal.

As the window rolled up, he waved good-bye. What about the happy meal?

After an hour, the air inside was getting stale. I pulled up the thick sleeve and checked my watch. Another three hours. I was about to take a quick break when I felt a tug on my leg. A cute toy poodle was attached to a leash attached to a very big man. I waved at the dog, then at its master. "Hey, buddy, want to try a Chicken Moma? Here's a coupon."

"I'm a vegetarian and so is my dog."

Vegetarian and horny, I bet. I glanced at the guy, who now had a broad smile, and attempted to shake the little guy off before he got off. "Hey!" I stuck my beak within inches of its face. "Find someone your own species."

The dog leaped off my leg and into his master's arms, shaking. "You scared him, you asshole!"

You're the asshole.

There were no exciting incidents after that and by noon, a few business types greeted me, then a guy who looked thirty years older than Junior.

"How's it going in there?" He pointed at the costume.

"Great," I lied, patting his hand. "Junior told me you were coming in."

"He has an appointment, so I'm filling in." He thumbed at the restaurant. "I'll be inside, so take a break when you're hungry or thirsty."

"Thanks." I wanted to tell him about my morning, but a car pulled up. "Catch you later, Bill."

After being mooned, I approached with caution. The front passenger window rolled down to reveal an elderly woman with a soft smile. "Can you tell me how to get to Dr. Fried's office?" She looked at a paper in her hand. "Something Indiantown Road."

"Seventy," the driver barked.

Did they really issue driver's licenses to centenarians?

"Seventy," she repeated, her smile fading. "I was told it's near your store."

"Hurry, we're late," he barked again.

Very old and very rude. I looked in both directions searching for a sign, but could only shrug. "Sorry."

The guy sped off. So much for courtesy.

"Hope you make your appointment!"

Around one thirty, I stepped inside for a much-needed break. The lunch rush was over, and I didn't see Bill, so I trudged to the men's room. My stomach was growling, and I couldn't wait to sink my teeth into a chicken fillet and fries. I was about to remove my beak when the toilet flushed. I decided to hold off until the guy left, but then another chicken guy emerged from the stall.

I blinked. "Hey, Bill, I didn't realize you were clowning around today. Got the late shift?"

"Don't make a move, dick face."

"Nice talk. You sound funny, Bill. Got a cold?"

The next thing I knew, my back was flat against the wall with a huge chicken blowing stale cigarette fumes in my face.

"You're not Bill, I take it."

"Don't ask no fucking questions."

Definitely not Bill. He pulled out a gun from I don't know where and shoved it under my beak. Instinctively, my arms sailed toward the ceiling. "I only make minimum wage, but you can take whatever I have in my pants pocket. I just have to take off the costume."

He grabbed my neck. "What are you, a wise ass? I want the register money, jerk-off."

I nodded. "Probably more than minimum wage in there," I squeezed out while choking.

The guy released his grip, and I felt something warm inside my costume. I would be happy to pay for the dry cleaning if I got out of here alive. I started shaking my leg to dry myself, but the guy pressed the gun into my stomach. I wasn't prone to suicide, so I stopped. I sneaked a peek at his feet; he didn't have my upgrade. Made sense, considering sneakers were better for bolting out the door.

"Open the door and step outside slowly." At least, that's what I thought he said through his costume. "And keep your hands in the air."

Bill was behind the counter and shot us a look as we single-filed toward him. He must have noticed the gun at the back of my head but didn't flinch.

"You okay, Eddie?"

"Shut your goddamn mouth and open the cash register."

That didn't come from me. Bill eased his hands in the air. "This can go very easy, so let's not get excited. Nobody needs to get hurt."

I didn't know if Bill was talking to me or my shadow. I nodded anyway.

"Don't tell me what the fuck to do! Just do what you're told."

"Whatever you say. You're in charge."

"Don't forget it, or this guy gets hurt."

I needed to shake my leg again.

Bill slowly reached into the cash register, removed a wad of bills, laid it on the counter, and stepped back. The evil chicken pushed me aside to scoop up the money. The costume didn't have pockets, so where was he going to stash it? He must have realized it and swore. At least, it sounded like a swear word. My nervous eyes shifted to his gun. Did the small puddle on the floor come from me? I glanced at Bill who must have noticed the same thing. A water pistol!

"Son of a bitch!" I leaped onto the chicken and pushed in his beak so he couldn't breathe. But he was more agile and aimed his gun at my beak. "Now I'm going to kill you." But he didn't pull the trigger, and I would have only gotten wet if he had. Instead, he charged for the door without the money.

Bill leaped over the counter, tripped on the corner, and fell on his face. Crazed, I chased after the chicken and yanked the bottom part of his outfit down to his ankles. He kicked and screamed until a cell phone went off. It sounded like the theme from The Sopranos. The guy dug inside his shorts to retrieve his phone. By then, Bill had recovered, and he took the opportunity to kick the guy in the balls. Forgetting the phone, the guy grabbed his manhood and howled.

The front door opened, and a business suit strolled in. "What the hell!"

I didn't let the chicken out of my grip. "The guy's trying to rob the place!"

He grabbed his cell from his suit pocket, punched in a quick number, and joined us by ripping off the chicken's head.

"Bastard!" the bad guy yelled.

Bill ran to the counter and returned with handcuffs. "Retirement present." He smiled and slapped them on the loser. "Wait till the guys hear about this!"

"Goddamn Chinese imitations." The headless chicken spit and kicked the toy gun away.

The cops showed up to find a thirty-something sitting on the floor, his outfit locked around his ankles and his blond hair in a messy spike.

Wait till Kate found out I was a hero!

OY VEY, MY NECK

Kate's face was filled with horror as I entered the house like a victorious warrior. She dashed over and locked her arms around my neck. I grimaced. "Thank God you're all right!"

"I'm fine, Kate, really." I attempted to peel back her arms as she trembled.

Between sniffles, she said, "And don't even think about going back there! It's too dangerous."

The pain in my neck suppressed a smile on my face. "Really, it was nothing."

She wiped her eyes. "It's all my fault. I pushed you out of the house."

Maybe I could milk this. "Don't blame yourself, Kate. I made the decision to go back to work." She was right, though: A few freebie meals didn't outweigh the risks. But I certainly wasn't about to let a robbery attempt stop my retirement plans, only my job title wasn't going to be Chicken Moma mascot.

The incident came with unexpected benefits. Bill and I became local heroes. Our pictures, sans costume, were splashed in the *Post* under the headline, "Attempted Chicken Robber's Plot Foiled." After Kate got over her shock, she treated me like a celebrity and offered herself, which I gladly accepted.

It was a hell of a short ride, waving wildly, and acting like a kid. But in retrospect, I realized how lonely life could be seeing the world incognito. Jesse once told me that shedding your skin was better than hiding inside it. I now got it.

Soon after the masked escapade, my missing golf partner, Joe, called me. An emergency had distracted him from our game, but was ready to join us the following week. But if Kate, who was treating my neck spasms with compresses and creams, didn't make my pain disappear soon, my buddies would have to play without me.

Bill, who also was licking his wounds from his fall, recommended a chiropractor. However, I was skeptical of people who jumped on bones for a living.

My family doctor didn't have an opening for a few days, so I settled for the chiropractor. I handed over my insurance card and filled out the usual forms. I slumped into a cushioned chair, glanced around, and stopped on a mounted TV showing a doctor—

presumed mine—performing chiropractic moves on a man in his thirties. I winced. I hope Bill was right about this guy.

Two other patients had arrived before me and appeared to be in a great deal of pain too. A woman in her forties wearing a cervical collar grimaced each time she turned a magazine page. A fifties-something guy in painter's overalls and a plaid shirt looked as though he was about to fall out of his chair. Would his body hold up until he was eligible to retire? His name was called, and he walked by listing port side. Poor bastard.

I closed my eyes, trying to keep my mind off the pain.

"Mr. Short?"

I rose too quickly and grunted. Inside the inner sanctum, I passed the likes of Mr. Lopsided who was no longer tipping over. Miracle doctor?

Doctor Baruška, a tall man in his fifties with a gray beard and mustache, reminded me of Sigmund Freud without the pipe. He introduced himself in a guttural accent and offered me a seat while he studied my skimpy file. When he finally closed it, he looked somber. "Mr. Short, I have to ask you an important question."

"Sure," I said with apprehension.

"Are you still using the same insurance company?"

"What? Yes, I gave the receptionist my card."

He flashed a smile. "Just kidding. The form says your pain is in the neck and shoulders and that it's moderate to severe."

I nodded too quickly and saw stars.

"And that you have no other history of pain. Do you know what caused this?"

I sucked in my chest with a bit of hubris and launched into detail. Prone to exaggeration, I extended my fifteen minutes of fame for the good doctor.

Dr. Baruška's eyes widened. "That was you? You were brave."

"And stupid."

He tugged at his beard. "Say, I could use you in my next film. Were you watching my video in the waiting room?"

I nodded.

"It's a few years old, and I want to update it. If I offered you the first five sessions for free, would you be interested in participating? It won't take long. . . . You'll be like an actor."

"Really?"

"Sure, I'll even bring in a makeup artist."

"Actor," I repeated.

"What do you say, Eddie? May I call you Eddie?"

We shook hands, and Dr. Baruška got down to business. He tenderly touched my neck and shoulders, but I flinched. He told me it most likely was muscular but wouldn't know until we took X-rays.

"I have to wait for treatment?"

He smiled reassuringly. "I'll have my massage therapist work out the kinks and alleviate some of the pain."

"Massage, that sounds great."

"I'll give you a prescription for the X-rays, and once we get the results back, probably in a few days, we can go from there." He winked. "We can finalize our movie business at the same time." He patted me on the shoulder. "Have my receptionist give you a form for the massage therapy."

Form for everything. The woman at the front desk pointed at another room down the hall. I nodded and began reading the form. "Excuse me, what's the name of the massage therapist?"

"Bruce Wang." She smiled.

I stepped back. "He's a guy?"

"An Asian guy."

I scratched my head. "Still, he's a guy?"

"He's very good. The patients love him."

I stepped forward and whispered, "It's just that I've never had a massage before. I always figured it would be, you know, a woman."

The receptionist offered a reassuring smile. "I can tell you once you've been Wanged, you'll never go elsewhere."

"Wanged?"

"That's what his patients affectionately call his massage. He's also straight."

I relaxed a bit. "Okay."

Bruce Wang was a slim man in his late thirties, neatly dressed in a T-shirt and Dockers. After introducing himself, he instructed me to remove my clothes.

"Everything but your shorts, then lie on the table, stomach down."

"All my clothes?" I asked.

"Except the shorts," he repeated. "I won't be covering those areas. Call me when you finish." He didn't laugh or wink, so I figured he was serious. Like Dr. Baruška, Wang had an accent. Did the American Chiropractic Association import its people? Not that I cared as long as the job got done.

I slowly removed my clothes, a bit distracted by taking in the tiny room. I dropped my shirt and slacks on a chair and noticed only one sheet spread across the table. I froze. Where was the top sheet? What if I got aroused? He might think I was gay. Should I tell him I'm not gay?

"You ready, Mr. Short?"

Of course, I wasn't ready. I grabbed a white jacket off a hook and slipped it on. "Ready."

Wang opened the door with a puzzled look.

"This for me?" I asked, waving my arms out of the sleeves.

He snickered. "No, that mine."

"Oh." I took it off and hung it back on the hook.

He pointed at the table. "You go there."

I nodded and climbed aboard, trying to banish negative thoughts. When my head was snug in the doughnut, Wang treated me to New Age music.

He touched my shoulders. "You tense, very tense. First time?"

I nodded into the doughnut.

"Ah, I take good care of you."

That's what I was afraid of.

"Just relax and listen to music, okay?"

I nodded again.

Wang told me he wouldn't work on my neck because of the pain. "Next time." He slowly applied the right pressure to my shoulders. No creams, just soft hands. The pain was almost ecstatic as his fingers pushed deep into my muscles, finding and destroying the knots. Go Wang! Finally, I relaxed . . . until he told me to turn over.

"Front?" I panicked but reluctantly turned over.

Wang worked my legs, thighs, and arms. "Too tense."

I clamped my eyes until he started working on my head. Then every touch, every stroke lulled me to near asleep. By the time the master's hands were done, I was floating.

"Finished. You get dressed now. I wait outside."

I wanted more Wang, but he disappeared. As I got dressed, I felt wobbly, drained.

"You okay?" he asked after returning.

I nodded. "Very."

"You drink plenty of water. It releases lactic acids. Okay?"

I nodded again.

"You come back?"

Oh, yeah. "I'll be back soon."

EBAY

Kate entered my cave to inform me about an eBay class at the community center.

"It would be perfect for you, Eddie," she said with a wide smile. "You can play on your computer, make money, and work in your underwear all at the same time." She threw in that it wasn't dangerous like my last endeavor.

I regarded Kate's smile, knowing she would do anything to save me from boredom. Considering I was on online and sitting in my underwear at the moment—not making any money—selling on eBay made sense. "Sounds interesting."

Kate's eyes settled on my head. "Not for nothing, Eddie, but you really need to do something about your hair."

"What's wrong with it?" I raked my fingers through the gray curls.

"For one thing, it needs combing. What if the FedEx guy knocks on the door, and I'm not home?"

I shrugged. "Don't answer?"

She shook her head and walked out of the room, leaving me to ponder my next venture. Navigating the Net was easy, but I never considered making a living from it. I leaned back in my chair and stared at my screensaver—a shot of Maui, Kauai, or some other Hawaiian island I couldn't remember—and considered my sales options. Kate's tchotchkes came to mind, but I would keep that to myself.

With imagination, you could sell anything on eBay. And because a sucker was born every minute, marketing was the key. I knew a guy who sold his girlfriend's worn boots online after she had tossed them in the garbage. He rubbed in a fresh coat of polish, buffed the tips, and showed his girlfriend. She thought he was crazy, of course, but then he mentioned money and eBay in the same breath. He asked her to model the boots so he could take a picture. "Men with foot fetishes would buy them in a heartbeat," he told her.

Our community center was filled with wannabe eBay entrepreneurs. I sat in the last row and counted heads, mostly gray like mine. The lights started flickering as though cueing a Broadway show. Within seconds, the lights cranked up, and a woman with hungry eyes and two assistants emerged from the shadows. The audience applauded.

"Who wants to make money?" she called out, pumping her fists in the air.

Hands flew up, including mine.

"Who wants to make lots of money?"

Both hands reached for the ceiling. Psyched.

"Sorry, you're in the wrong class."

Sighs.

"Who wants to leave?"

No one raised a hand.

She savored a smile. "Right choice, folks. I'm going to show you how to make money and have fun doing it. Some of you will do better than others, but no one is going to get rich." She surveyed the room and smiled again. "At least, not overnight."

An assistant turned on a projector and started a PowerPoint presentation, the name Candy Mars lighting up the screen. I snickered, must be her eBay stage name. Candy, slightly overweight in her late forties with teased bleached blond hair, was dressed in a white blouse and a skirt that appeared tailored for a smaller woman. Her white face was blotched with what looked like pancake batter.

She introduced herself and her assistants, who turned out to be her children with normal names like Susie and Andy, both in their early twenties. Candy opened by telling us she'd been selling on eBay for eight years and emphasized she'd made enough money to provide a comfortable life, but not enough to upgrade her lifestyle. Put another way, don't give up our day jobs.

After bursting our get-rich bubble, Candy started working the room like a salesperson on steroids. Was she getting paid by the syllable? While Susie handed out folders, Andy continued the PowerPoint. I took notes and tried to catch every fourth word even as Candy assured us all the information was in the handouts. My brain was on overload concocting a screen name and mulling what I could sell and how much. My neighbor touched my arm with his gnarled finger. "You get what she said about the fees?"

His aquiline nose reminded me of my grandfather's, and he looked old enough to have retired twice. "Insertion fees?" I asked.

"I don't know. She was talking about fees."

"There are a few." I paged through my notes. "She said everything's in her handout."

He nodded, but a few minutes later, he tapped me on the shoulder. "What did she say about shipping?"

I pointed at the blue pocket portfolio. "It's in there," I whispered.

"I'm hard of hearing." He pointed at his ear. "My batteries are dying."

Ah, that explained it. I smiled sympathetically and shifted. Had he bought his batteries on eBay?

People usually took a class to learn, meet people, or kill time. I guessed my friend here was in the last camp.

"Morris," he said, extending his hand.

I shook it quickly. "Eddie."

"Eddie, you look like my son."

The distraction annoyed me, but I smiled. "He must be good looking."

"Was. He died."

"Oh gee, I'm sorry."

His eyes grew heavy.

"You two in the back. Are you interested in learning about eBay or not?"

I glanced around, then realized Candy was admonishing us. "Hearing problems." I pointed at Morris.

"What did she say?" Morris asked. I gestured a zipping motion across the mouth to him. "Sorry, teacher, my hearing aid isn't working."

The class roared, but Candy's frosty expression reminded me of Kate's when she wasn't pleased with excuses. "We're on a tight schedule, so please refrain from talking."

Nothing like being back in school.

Candy's lecture turned out to be informative, and I was ready to sell my first item: anything of Kate's. Candy advised us not to get discouraged if we didn't sell right away.

I was about to leave when Morris tugged on my pants. "You doing anything?" he asked with a doleful look.

"What did you have in mind?"

He cupped his hand to his ear, so I leaned in to repeat the question.

His eyes were hopeful. "Lunch, perhaps."

I shrugged. "Sure, why not?"

"But I need to pick up a battery first, or you'll be talking to yourself." We smiled.

Morris suggested a sports bar sporting young waitresses with big chests and tight shorts. As we entered, my eyes attempted to stay polite. "My favorite place," Morris said as we slid into a booth. "It makes me feel young."

Or horny! His wife died about two years ago, I learned, soon after a heart attack killed his son. "He was only fifty three," Morris said.

I nodded sympathetically. Was my outing with Morris going to throw me back into a depression?

"Last year was tough," he said, barely audible. "This year, I started taking classes just to get out of the house."

I nodded again, empathizing for Morris and pondering my own mortality. The waitress approached and waved at Morris.

"Hey, good looking." She smiled. At least, I thought she smiled. "I see you brought along a friend."

"This is my nephew."

While she studied us, I studied her surreptitiously. "Right. I see the resemblance."

We ordered wings and beer, and Morris turned back after watching her go. "My son and nephew looked alike."

"Hey, I'm honored. Besides, I haven't been a nephew since my aunt and uncle died."

I squeezed in a few retirement questions to get a sense from an experienced retiree. After Morris left the workforce about the same age as me, he grew restless and began brainstorming things to do. Like me, he didn't have any hobbies, and like Kate, his wife didn't want him around the house.

"The 24/7 syndrome," I said. "I'm familiar with it."

"Don't get me wrong, Eddie, Blanche and I loved each other, but our interests changed over the years. By the time our son moved into his own place, we ran out of things to talk about. . . . I'm not into sports, and I don't read very much, so for me, it was difficult finding an outlet. . . . Most of my friends were still working, so I saw them only on occasion."

Ms. Silicones returned with the beers, and I downed a much-needed slug. "I volunteered for years, reading to the blind, stuff like that," he said. "It gave me enormous satisfaction helping people."

I nodded. “My son suggested the idea. At some point, I want to find something meaningful.”

Morris smiled. “Let me know, I have connections.”

I let a few moments pass. “So, are you going to be selling anything on eBay?”

“Me? Nah. I just like to keep my mind sharp. You?”

“Maybe, I haven’t decided yet. It didn’t appear the average Joe could make real money anyway. It would just be passing time, I’m afraid.”

“I don’t have much to sell,” Morris said wistfully. “I gave away most of Blanche’s stuff.”

I nodded thoughtfully. I could tell his wife still pervaded his mind. Our lunch arrived, and I took a few quick bites and washed it down with my beer.

“I hope I’m not depressing you, Eddie. I mean, sickness and death.”

I finished a wing and licked my fingers. “It sounds like the worst is behind you, Morris. That’s good.”

He nodded. “I hope we can be friends.”

I picked up another wing. “I’m sure we can.”

Morris started playing with his food, and I asked if everything was all right.

He stopped. “I met someone.”

“Really? That’s great.”

"She's a neighbor and very nice. She helps me get through the day."

Morris didn't mention her name, so I suspected he felt guilty. "We all need someone, Morris. Life is too short."

He leaned in, glanced around, then back at me. "I think we're going to do it."

Do it! Was Morris asking for my approval? "Sure, great."

"I haven't mentioned this to anyone."

I hoped his girlfriend knew about his plans.

His eyes averted mine. "Do you think it's right, Eddie? It's been a couple of years since Blanche passed, and well, time is moving quickly."

I hadn't advised anyone on sex since Jesse was fifteen, and as it turned out, Jesse knew more than I did. "Gee, Morris, it's a personal decision, but I don't think you should feel guilty about it, if that's what you're worried about."

He looked down and fell silent.

"You seem to care about this woman, right?"

He glanced up and nodded slowly.

"And she's obviously into you."

More nods.

I downed my beer and wiped my mouth with a paper napkin. "I say go for it."

Morris reached for my hand and shook it. "Thanks, Eddie." He smiled with a degree of satisfaction. "I don't need pills either."

"Even better."

"Use it or lose it."

"I'll remember that." I definitely didn't want to lose it.

After a few minutes of silence, Morris asked to be excused.

"Sure, I'll join you. Drinking does that to me."

He held out a hand. "I mean to meet my friend."

Horny bastard. "Sure."

"Jenny is probably wondering where I am."

I offered him my cell, and he punched in her number. His conversation sounded formal, and I attempted not to listen, but he finally said, "Me too."

"Thanks, Eddie." He handed back my phone. "Jenny was a little worried. Can't wait to tell her about you."

I smiled, yearning for another chance to spend quality time with my father.

"How about we make this a regular thing?" he asked.

"I'd like that, Morris."

The waitress dropped off the bill, and Morris beat me to it. "Let me," I protested.

"No way, Eddie."

"Okay, I'll get the next one."

Morris's soft smile reminded me of a cherub. "That's why we'll meet again—so we'll be even."

DOCTORS, DENTISTS, AND DEPRESSED FRIENDS

Growing up, I didn't recall my mother suffering from anything more than a common cold. Even in early retirement, she complained only about the flu, which she attributed to a flu shot. So I became alarmed when, living in Florida, she sent me a list of her dozen or so doctors. "In case of an emergency," she wrote at the bottom.

I called her in a panic. "Mom, I just received your list. When did you start seeing a heart specialist?"

Her silence intensified my fears. "Mom, are you there?"

"Eddie, I'm thinking. Which doctor was that, darling?"

I thumbed down the page. "Dr. Harris."

"Harris, Harris. Oh, him. Janice recommended him. She likes Dr. Harris a lot."

I gripped the phone. "Yeah, but why are you seeing him?"

More silence.

"Mom?"

"I'm thinking. Dr. Harris ran a battery of tests and told me I have a slight heart murmur."

"Of course, you have a murmur." My voice elevated. "You've had it all your life. . . . Has it been bothering you?"

My mother had been flighty as long as I could remember, so her brain and tongue didn't always synch. She took a few moments to answer. "Thank God, no, Eddie."

I relaxed. "Then why the appointment?"

A loud commotion in the background prompted her to snap at my stepfather, something about turning down the damn television.

"Sorry, Eddie. Your stepfather must have forgotten to put his hearing aid in this morning. What was the question?"

"Heart murmur."

"Right. Janice has one too. That's why she goes to Dr. Harris. We were talking about—"

"Who is this Dr. Schlemiel?"

"Schlemmer, Eddie, his name is Schlemmer."

"Whatever. It says he's an ENT specialist. That's an ear, nose, and throat guy. So which are you going to him for?" This ought to be good.

Another pause. "It was just a precautionary visit."

When I mentioned her family doctor was the first line of defense, she assured me he too was on her list.

"So it was his idea to send you to the specialist?"

Mother giggled. "Of course not. It was Janice's."

I rolled my eyes. "Please tell me why you're seeing all these other doctors." My brain was crying out for relief. Would Medicare be around for the rest of us? "And please don't tell me they're nice and that Janice recommended all of them."

"They are nice, except for Dr. Pullman."

My finger searched the page. "Pullman? I don't see his name on the list."

"That's because I don't see him anymore."

I rubbed my temples. "What happened?"

"Well, for one thing, he was too abrupt and never seemed to have time for me."

"And the second?"

"Funny, son."

Her doctor, or rather former doctor, probably tired of my mother's line of questioning. She apparently was relentless, especially after the good doctor claimed nothing was wrong with her.

"What kind of doctor is he anyway?"

"I don't remember. It was a while ago."

"Christ, no wonder our health premiums are skyrocketing."

"There's no reason to swear, Eddie. Besides, don't you want your mother healthy?"

Defeated, I read off the rest of the names, half of which I couldn't pronounce, and stopped at the last one. "Since when do you have back problems?"

Silence.

"Mom?"

She whispered into the phone as though my stepfather, without his hearing aid in the next room, actually might hear her. "That would be Dr. Wallace. He's a chiropractor. . . . Your stepfather is always complaining about his back."

I snickered. "From what, opening the car door for you and your lady friends after chauffeuring you back and forth to doctors?"

"You're not very funny, Eddie. But if you must know, he pulled it one night while we were having sex."

Christ. "Let's change the subject."

"Well, Mr. Health, you asked."

While my mother took extreme measures to monitor her health, maybe she was on to something. Aging should make us more vigilant in fighting sickness and death; it was all around us. But outside of my morbid fascination with the obituaries, I never thought of death as imminent. Maybe that was before retirement.

Lately, I zeroed in on any article about annual examinations, cholesterol tests, X-rays and prostrate exams. Didn't you just hate when the doctor …? I even read about mammograms and pap smears—for Kate, of course.

While we needed to eat right, not smoke, control our blood pressure, and reduce our cholesterol, the bottom line? Genes—good or bad. That was the dominate factor as to when our maker would take us. The other stuff was secondary.

And let's not forget the dentist. A visit might show telltale signs, such as oral cancer and gum disease. I'd had gum problems before, so I visited my dentist every three months.

And today was that day. I was about to turn on the car when my cell started singing. I didn't have time to put on my glasses to see who it was, so I answered it. What a mistake. Now I was in for a long, depressing ride to the dentist.

"Eddie, it's Neal," he said, subdued.

"Neal, are you okay?" I started the engine, swearing in my head. I hadn't spoken to Neal in almost a year—with good reason. He was one of those unfortunate souls who didn't know they suffered from depression. He acted as though he hauled around Quasimodo's hump, which meant everyone around him was susceptible to depression.

"Evelyn left me."

Did I mention he was also direct? "Gee, Neal, I'm sorry to hear that. What happened?"

A few sniffles. “She said she got fed up with my moodiness.”

That was a diplomatic way to put it.

“She was always complaining that I was bringing her down.”

And everyone else within earshot. “But you guys have been married forever.”

“Twenty-nine years. And to think, I was about to retire.”

Bingo! Neal broke down as he mentioned Evelyn moving out to rent an apartment. “I really thought we were happy.”

Did Neal even know what happy meant?

“We had plans—travel, cruises …”

And plenty of time for Evelyn to be subjected to Neal’s depression 24/7. Not good.

“She was always online looking for vacation packages.”

It started to click, but I said, “There are great deals online, Neal. Patience is the name of the game.”

“Yeah, but in the middle of the night? . . . I caught her in one of those chat rooms, probably talking to some guy.”

The marriage was dead.

“She tried telling me it was a travel club where people talk about trips and recommend places.”

I could only imagine. “Sounds innocent enough.”

“It was bullshit! She’s probably gonna run off with some guy to Europe.”

Depressed and angry, a hell of a cocktail. “Neal, I think you’re getting ahead of yourself. She probably just needs a little space.”

"She signed a year's lease." He was wailing as he hung up.

I'd been seeing the same family doctor and dentist since moving to South Florida in the mid-eighties. So when friends advised me to seek a family doctor closer to my new home in case of an emergency, I wasn't ready to give up my regulars because I was so comfortable with them. I didn't mind driving an hour to see them.

I remembered the last visit with my hygienist, Betty Leahy, a flaming redhead in her mid-thirties. "Give me a big smile, Eddie," she said with open arms.

It was Betty's standard line. I obliged as she tugged on my chin and popped her finger into my mouth to move around my tongue. Or was that my uvula? She finished her tricks by pulling my lips back and smiled. "Nice and pink."

We hadn't even made it to the exam room yet. I searched the waiting room, waiting for a standing ovation.

"Come," she said, grabbing my arm to lead me to her workstation. I'd known Betty since she graduated from hygienist school back in the nineties. In fact, I was her first patient.

I folded myself into the chair and waited for Betty to bark out the usual: Anything different from the last visit? Aches and pains? Bleeding?

No, thank goodness.

"You're too easy. Come on, Eddie, give me something I can work with."

I smiled then asked Betty how she was getting along since her recent bitter divorce. After stuffing my mouth with cotton, she had spewed, "Bastard, I could have gotten AIDS or something worse."

Worse than AIDS?

She had caught my expression and waved her hand. "Don't worry, Eddie, the test came back negative."

I nodded in relief.

Her eyes raged on. "While he was out with his friend, I ransacked the house and removed everything but my wedding dress. Maybe he'll give it to his lover, or sell it on eBay for all I care." She flashed a smile. "I closed out all the bank accounts."

I snuck a look at her hands, hoping they were steady.

"Open your mouth wider!" The double-ended dental probe glinted at me.

I hoped Betty realized I wasn't what's his face. She wasn't delicate with my gums, but I refrained from complaining. When she seemingly was satisfied with the one-way conversation, she barked another order. "You can rinse when you want to."

I spit out blood and residue. "Another woman is tough," I said in a sympathetic tone.

"Who said anything about a woman?"

For today's visit, I hoped Betty left the divorce in the waiting room.

"You like retirement, Eddie? You and Kate?" She snapped on her latex gloves.

I squeezed my shoulders. "So far, so good."

Her index finger poked my chest playfully. "Good, keep it that way. It's important."

I nodded and opened my mouth like a trained monkey.

"All men should be like you, Eddie. You listen." She laughed.

I tried to smile, but her fingers were crawling in my mouth. I usually closed my eyes on cue, Betty had a glow about her.

She caught me staring. "What?" she asked.

"Yu luk gud."

She removed her fingers. "English, Eddie."

"You look happy."

She smiled. "You think so?"

"Absolutely. What gives?"

She leaned in. "I have a new man in my life."

I gave her some teeth. "That's great."

"You'll never guess how we met."

"Online dating?"

Betty lifted an eyebrow. "How did you know …?"

"Most popular way to meet people these days."

She nodded absently. “So, you think it’s a good idea?”

I shrugged and thought about Neal’s news. “I’m not an expert, but I hear it works.”

She let a few moments pass. “I can’t wait to meet him.”

I suppressed a confused look. “You mean see him?”

Betty shook her head. “We’ve been emailing each other. He’s flying in from Chicago this weekend.”

I turned up my bottom lip. “Chicago? That’s quite a distance, Betty.”

She savored a smile. “He’s being transferred to Fort Lauderdale. Perfect, no?”

“I guess. But you haven’t met him yet.”

“Maybe not in the flesh, but I feel like I’ve known him for years. We talk on the phone for hours. Want to see a picture of him?”

Whether I wanted to or not, she pulled a glossy out of her uniform pocket and shoved it under my nose. “What do you think?”

I pushed her hand back for a better look. I chuckled. Typical headshot. “Is he an actor?”

“I thought so too,” she said, admiring the photograph. “His name is Barry. He’s a computer geek.”

I nodded. “Well, good luck, Betty.”

“Thanks.” She tucked the photo back into her uniform. “You can rinse when you want to.”

GAMBLING WITH EX-RELATIVES

I knew about little old ladies gambling their social security away. But were they trying to make ends meet, or just breaking the boredom? Either could happen in retirement. For me, I hit the jackpot more than thirty years ago.

Kate was never a gamble, but you might ask her what she thought about gambling. As for boredom, that's another issue.

Kate had been giggling on the phone like a schoolgirl for the past thirty minutes. After hanging up, she entered my cave all excited. "Jenny wants to meet me at the Hard Rock Casino to play Texas Hold'em."

My eyes shifted from the computer. "That sounds like fun. How about I join you?"

Her face fell. "Gee, Eddie, it's kind of girls night out. Besides…"

"What?"

"Nothing. I don't want to discuss it." She started for the door.

"Hold on a second." I rolled back my chair. "Nothing never means nothing. Let's have it."

Kate stopped before grabbing the doorknob and turned around. "It's just that I haven't played before."

"And . . .?"

She looked at the floor. "I know you'll criticize me."

"Kate, whatever gave you that idea?" When she didn't answer, I said, "Look, I'll teach you how to play."

She grimaced. "I don't think that's a good idea, Eddie."

"Why not? I'm a good player. A little rusty, maybe . . ."

Kate fixed her eyes on me. "If you want to know the truth, I'm not crazy about you teaching me."

My mouth dropped. "How can you say that? I'm a great teacher."

"With other people maybe." I could tell she was trying to stay calm. "Remember the time you tried teaching me how to drive? We almost got a divorce."

"Kate, that was over thirty years ago. Besides, I can't remember that far back."

Kate nodded rapidly. "That's because you don't want to remember. You kept yelling at me, and when you wouldn't let up, I stopped the car in the middle of the road and got out. Remember that, Mr. Teacher?"

I raised a hand. "Oh, come on, I wasn't yelling. I was merely trying to make a point."

She raised an eyebrow. "You were downright mean!"

My wife obviously hadn't left the scene of the incident, so I softened my tone and promised I would be more understanding this time.

"I should have listened to my friends. They had the same experience with their husbands."

The bait. "I thought you didn't want to discuss it."

"I don't. Why do you think I don't like to drive when you're in the car?"

"You like my driving better?"

She scowled. I offered an olive branch. "I apologize again. Let's start over."

"It's too late, Eddie. I already have my license."

"I meant poker."

Kate remained silent for a moment. "Only if you promise to be nice."

I hopped off the chair to hug her. "Come on, poker is easier than driving."

She pulled back. "No yelling, or I quit."

I searched my desk for a deck of cards and met Kate at the kitchen table. It felt good working the cards again, and Kate seemed impressed with my shuffling. I threw in some card tricks before dealing out five-card stud.

Kate studied her cards and glanced at mine. "What does it mean when you have three queens and I don't have a pair?"

I smiled. "It means we should be playing strip poker."

You could pick your friends but not your ex-relatives. And Billy Watson was one ex-brother-in-law who Kate wished I'd forget about. He was married to Kate's older sister, Laura, for fifteen years, and everyone but Laura knew they were mismatched from the start. So it wasn't much of a surprise when Billy strayed and their marriage dissolved. Despite Kate's disapproval, Billy and I had stayed in touch.

Billy retired a year ago after almost forty years with the phone company and started saving money the old-fashioned way: clipping coupons and buying wholesale.

At least, he and Kate had something in common, but nobody beat Billy's tenacity at saving a buck. Plus, he loved sharing deals with his friends. His "specials" even clogged up my e-mail sometimes.

Kate was unusually quiet as we traveled south on I-95 toward Billy's house in Boca Raton, and it had nothing to do with me winning strip poker.

"He'll feel bad if you don't at least say hello," I said.

She stared straight ahead. "He'll get over it."

Sometimes Kate seemed to take the divorce worse than her sister. I stopped the car a few doors from Billy's house for her to hop into the driver's seat. She made an exception to drive a hundred feet with me as a passenger.

"You can't avoid him forever." I said.

Kate pulled up to Billy's house and snapped her head at me. "Do me a favor, Eddie. Make sure he doesn't take you to the Hard Rock."

I chuckled. "Relax, Kate, I don't think they offer coupons."

She nodded. "Knowing him, it's probably some topless place, so behave yourself."

I held her hand and played with her wedding ring. "Kate, Billy cheated on your sister. I'm not Billy."

She rubbed my hand softly and smiled. "I know. It's just that he's a bad influence."

I wanted to assure Kate that Billy was more inclined these days to charm the pants off a cashier with his coupons than a stripper. Instead, I kissed her good-bye.

"He's by the door," Kate blurted, pushing me out of the car.

"He's not going to bite." I tripped over my shoes, then looked up and saw Billy waving wildly. I waved back for both of us.

Kate rolled down the window to warn me to be outside Billy's house alone at midnight, or I was walking home.

"Yes, ma'am, and good luck at the Hard Rock."

Billy watched the car pull away. "Too bad Kate had other plans."

"Maybe next time."

Billy ushered me into his family room. "What do you think?" he said like a proud parent.

I whistled. "Nice."

"A 55-inch Samsung 1080p 120Hz Smart LED TV," he said in one breath. "Forty percent off."

My eyes followed a hiker crossing a crevasse on Mount Everest. "Look at those colors! And the clarity. That's the Discovery Channel, right?"

"Think so. And I got them to deliver it free."

Did I mention Billy's favorite color was green? "So, what did you have in mind?"

He broke into a wide grin. "It's a birthday surprise."

I looked confused. "My birthday isn't for another six months."

Billy shrugged. "Maybe not yours, but somebody has a birthday today." He checked his watch. "Come on, birthday boy, let's go."

Fifteen minutes later Billy pulled up to the Boca Raton Marriott and searched for a spot. "Must be a convention going on," I said. "Or a concert. Did you get tickets, Billy?"

Billy was too busy looking for parking to respond.

"There." I pointed.

Billy squeezed his white Camry between two SUVs. "We gotta hurry," he said, sprinting ahead.

When I caught up, Billy was standing in a long line. "What's going on?" I asked out of breath.

He mumbled something unintelligible. Somehow it didn't seem like a concert. When we reached the front, a middle-aged woman in a business suit smiled and asked for a name.

"Quinn," Billy said with a nervous smile.

She checked her list and glanced up. "It says three, Mr. Quinn, one couple and a single."

He gave me a side-glance, then back to her with doleful eyes. "She came down with the flu."

"Oh." She scrutinized us, checked her list again, and motioned over a large athletic type.

I nudged Billy. "What the hell is going on?"

"There must be a slight misunderstanding."

We followed the jock to a corner. He turned and smiled politely. "Gentlemen, the program requires that both spouses be present. . . . Unless you're single."

Billy assured him that he was single.

The guy's smile cooled a notch. "Then you can stay." He turned to me. "You're more than welcome to come back another time with your wife. Sorry, but that's our policy."

Billy shook his head. "You're missing an opportunity. My friend here is interested in your product tonight."

The guy folded his massive arms. Was that a tattoo of the entire United States on his arm? He turned to me. "Look, I don't make the rules. We have presentations every couple of months. I'm sure you and your wife . . ."

"I'm sorry, did you say presentation?" I asked.

Mr. Universe scowled. "He doesn't know?"

Billy shrugged. "It was a surprise. I hadn't told him yet."

The guy's veins in his neck were throbbing. "It's a fractional ownership presentation."

I backed away with big eyes as though surrounded by lepers. "Time share!"

"Absolutely not," he said, waving me off. "This is an upgraded vacation program. We have exotic resorts all over the world."

I stabbed Billy in the chest with my finger. "I can't believe you did this. And if Kate were here, we'd both be toast."

"So I guess the dinner and gift are out tonight?" Billy asked seriously.

I bolted for the door, wishing I had my own car. I waited more than ten minutes by his car, wondering if Mr. Universe was crushing my ex-brother-in-law's head, which was fine by me. But when Billy showed up, he was smiling.

I shook my head. "You got balls. You embarrassed the shit out of me back there."

He rested his hand on my shoulder. "Come on, Eddie, I thought it would be fun."

"You thought it would be free. No wonder Laura divorced you."

"It wasn't because of good deals."

I opened the door. "Let's get the hell out of here."

"Wait a second. Don't you want to know where I've been?"

I threw up my hands. "Billy, I really don't give a damn."

He pulled a nametag out of his pants' pocket and handed it to me. "For you."

"Who the hell is Edward Harrison?"

That infamous smile. "I hear you're looking to enhance your stock portfolio, Mr. Harrison."

I stepped back. "Please don't tell me you found another presentation."

"Eddie, hear me out. Wouldn't you rather have filet mignon instead of those finger sandwiches we would have been stuck with?"

"Why me?" I moaned.

He led me by my elbow to another conference area. "Talk about luck," he said. "They're offering a free financial seminar, and the poor Harrisons had to cancel, so they're letting us take their place. I told the guy we had big portfolios that needed tweaking."

I shook my head. "You're killing me."

He pinned Rose Harrison's nametag to his shirt and gave me a peck on my cheek.

ON THE COUCH

I finally decided to dip my toes into therapy. I believed it was overkill, but Jesse thought otherwise. Made sense; he was a therapist. He had recommended solution-focused brief therapy (SFBT). Say what? Jesse explained it was future-focused, goal-directed therapy that focused on solutions, instead of the problems. Say what?

Okay, in layman's terms, SFBT's approach assumes clients have an idea of what would make their lives better, but they may not be able to articulate the details. Hence, the therapist helps brainstorm the solutions. Got it?

For example, I knew I wanted to enjoy myself but didn't know how. The therapist's role was to guide me by asking questions focusing on the present or the future, on the premise that problems were best solved by identifying what was already working, instead of harping on the past or origin of the problem. So what specifically was working for me?

Knowing me, Jesse wouldn't suggest some long-term therapy that cracked open the doors to my past. Let the demons rot in the cobwebs of my brain, which they had over the years. That's not to say I didn't need long-term therapy; most of us do. But at my age and juncture in life, my son believed SFBT would help me by focusing on the what-now syndrome. I'm sure he was tiring of me complaining every time we were together, so I finally submitted.

Unlike a massage, I wanted a male therapist, perhaps my age, about sixty. After all, men knew men better than women knew men. Though according to Kate, she knew me all too well, but you get my point. I gave Jesse strict orders not to pair me with one of his colleagues. Despite the confidentially rule, I felt better with someone outside my son's drinking buddies. There was nothing like being the center of discussion of old Eddie Short.

Therapy day arrived. Malcom Summers, a psychotherapist for more than twenty-five years, was a friend of a friend of Jesse's colleague—in other words, twice removed—who specialized in guys like me who thought retirement would be a cakewalk. At fifty-five, Dr. Summers fit my age request, and I liked that he was a doctor. Thankfully, I was the only one in his waiting room, which he shared with another shrink. God forbid I should see someone I knew. Then again, they'd probably be embarrassed too.

I anxiously thumbed through an *AARP* magazine without reading a single article, then swapped it for *Senior* magazine and did the same thing. I was reaching for yet another magazine when the door to the inner sanctum opened. Out walked a guy my age, all smiles. Good sign.

After Mr. Smiles left, another man appeared, presumably my doctor. He too smiled. Contagious? We introduced ourselves, and he ushered me into his office where I darted for the couch.

"Mr. Short, may I call you Ed?"

I dug into the couch and turned to Malcom the Shrink. "No."

"No?"

I smiled. "Eddie, please. My father was Ed, and I sure don't want to be associated with him." Reading Malcom's expression, I shut up. Oh God, don't suggest long-term therapy. "Actually, Dad was given that name by his father, and I thought it was too formal for me … what am I talking about? My father and I didn't have a great relationship. Can we just do the SFBT thing?"

"Of course, Eddie. That's what we spoke about over the phone. We'll leave your dad where you left him off . . . unless you wish to include him in one of our sessions at some point."

"He's dead, but fair enough."

"Before we get started, Eddie, the couch is for my naps." He smiled and pointed at a chair facing another chair facing a photo of . . . Sigmund himself, not smiling. "This works better for all my clients. I wouldn't want you falling asleep on me."

Funny. "I guess I wanted to get an idea how it might have worked with Freud." I pointed at the photograph and adjusted the chair slightly away from somber Freud and waited for Malcom—definitely on a first-name basis. He dropped his slight frame into his chair and adjusted it in line with mine. Malcom had a soft face, few wrinkles, sincere smile, and lots of gray hair in a ponytail. Maybe he'd been a rock star.

We faced each other, mano a mano. "So, Eddie, I understand you'd like to discuss the changes in your life since retirement. I never met your son, Jesse, but he's a colleague of a friend of mine and asked that he find you the right therapist. I've been working with clients—that's what some of us call patients. It's more informal. That's the way I like to involve myself, as informal as possible. It also should help eliminate the angst of traditional therapy, those long-term sessions as you alluded to before.

I didn't respond, so he continued. "I've been working with pre and post retirees for a number of years, and many, if not most, have the same … issue. Loss."

"Loss? I'm not lost. I'm … finding my way."

Malcom tented his fingers, nodded. "That's a good sign. Tell me more."

"When I worked, I felt productive, sometimes important. Well, not at the end of my career but certainly over the years. Now, not so much. I mean, there aren't any challenges left. . . . Well, there is one: staying out of my wife's hair. I try."

Malcom remained deadpan, so I figured he meant for me to continue. "I can't keep myself busy. Time is all I have, and there's too much of it. Jesse believes I should volunteer or get a part-time job—you don't want to hear about my last part-time gig—or go back to school. . . . Like I said, my wife wants me out of her hair."

Finally, a smile.

"Her day fills up without so much as a thought. She has projects inside and outside the house, and I still manage to get in her way. Did I mention I'm on medication for low serotonin levels? I mean, that's a good thing, right?"

A nod. "Yet, you're here."

"Right, Jesse's idea. He believes I need to work out my … time." I leaned forward. "I realized he was right when I continued taking naps every afternoon I wasn't doing anything, which was pretty much every day. I mean, even I can't stay on the Internet all day. Don't get me wrong, I could, but I was running out of sites, and there's millions out there. Oh yeah, I took up golf, a present from my wife—another story—but I got bored and was going to sell the bag and clubs online but thought twice. I mean, it was a present. And that reminds me, I took an eBay course. Not bad, made a friend who's eighty-something and sleeping with a new woman. Well, he's widowed, so I told him to go for it. . . . Where was I?"

"eBay?"

"Right. I couldn't sell very much. Hell, when we moved to Juno Beach, I got rid of most of my stuff. Probably should have kept my winter clothes; they sell well up North. I finally sold my fly-fishing book and rod. Lost interest before I started. Kate agreed, given it was just taking up space in our tiny townhouse. . . . . And there's my brother-in-law, former, actually. I mean, he's satisfied clipping coupons all day. I don't cut coupons; Kate does."

"Eddie?"

"Yes."

"We don't have to squeeze everything into one session, but I do see where you're going with this."

"You do, really?" I smiled with hope.

Malcolm nodded. "You've got a lot going on in your head, and you're trying to sort out your life. So our goal is to get you focused and find a few interesting hobbies that make you happy, maybe productive. Make sense?"

"I think so. I'm OK then? I mean, I'm not going bonkers or anything? Jesse didn't think so, but he's my son and loves me. But I'm paying you, so I figure you'd tell me the truth."

Malcolm laughed.

"What?"

"You're fine, Eddie. Try to relax. This is going to be fun."

FINK

I never would bet against Robert Fink. Fink—he retired his first name in high school—was my oldest childhood friend and a wheeler-dealer by every sense of the word. He had the Midas touch in almost every business venture he entered. Fink gambled on life—and death. He knew his place in the world, but accepted no limitations. What he lacked in academic credentials, he overcompensated with street smarts. Did I mention Fink made lots of money?

Fink came from humble beginnings. His parents were struggling Irish immigrants raising two kids, which left an indelible mark on his psyche. (His father changed the family name from Finnk.) Fink was convinced he was one step away from the city projects, but that motivated him.

Fink and I met in a Catholic elementary school where his parents sacrificed to provide him with a religious education. Even back then, Fink was more interested in the almighty dollar than learning the Gospel.

We gravitated toward each other probably because of our economic similarities. My father started drinking heavily when I was five, soon after his dominating mother died, and he couldn't hold a job. So my mother worked two jobs and was never home when I returned from school. Though I wasn't a latchkey kid—my father was usually asleep or in a stupor when I got home—I too felt the projects were too close for comfort. At times, my father fought valiantly to quit the juice, as he had fighting the Japanese in Tarawa, spending his initial dry periods in VA hospitals throughout the state. On his last stay at the Montrose campus in upstate New York, he died of a heart attack at the ripe old age of fifty.

While Fink's personality was driven by abject poverty, he had a stable and loving family. I lost half of my immediate family to alcohol, the other to codependency. Driven wasn't in my blueprint; avoidance was. The thought of taking risks paralyzed me. But perhaps I inherited some of my mother's depth, which Fink lacked. And that difference in our personalities was the catalyst to melding a lifelong friendship.

After a year in a Catholic high school, we didn't want to continue, so we wound up in the same New York City school. My mother, exhausted from her difficult life, nevertheless pushed me, and I worked hard to get accepted to City College. Fink was too busy working nights to concentrate on school, finding solace in making a buck. He never had a propensity—he liked that word—for education and never pursued college. But he was anything but dumb and made and saved more money during high school than I did for years following college.

I pushed Fink to finish high school, competing with his nights sweeping a warehouse floor at a tool and die company. Fortunately, he ingratiated himself with the owner who hired him full time after high school and soon promoted him to foreman. A few years later, the owner died, and not having a family, left the business to Fink, which proved college wasn't for everyone. A bit of luck didn't hurt either.

As a result of Fink's work ethic, he didn't have time for a wife. In fact, he didn't have time for two ex-wives, but he adored his mother. He became a successful businessman who branched out in other ventures. I stopped asking him which ventures years ago, and he never asked me for an IRS get-out-of-jail card.

A few years back, Fink decided to buy a small condo in Miami as a test for real estate projects in South Florida. He offered to pay me a management fee to take care of it for him, but I declined on the condition he include me in his plans. But Fink had planned to offer me a quarter interest in the venture anyway.

I worked with a Realtor, a middle-aged woman named Joan Wiggins, who found us tenants. I lived an hour north of Miami, so I decided to introduce myself to the couple by phone. John and

Silvia Moore with their two little Moores became the quintessential perfect tenants. They paid on time, never called in the middle of the night, and kept the place immaculate.

Unfortunately, John died in his sleep a week before their lease came up for renewal, leaving his family enough money for a down payment on a house. The all-American dream: save, die, a house for the widow.

"If it hadn't been for my husband dying, I would have never been able to afford it," Silvia said with an accent heavily spiced with Spanish. "Poor John, he had a bad heart."

"Yes, poor John," I said.

"He left me with only a modest insurance policy."

He also left her with one less mouth to feed.

A week before moving, Silvia called up panting, her accent even heavier.

"Mr. Short! Lightning struck my living room window and blew out my new TV. It was scary. . . . Who's responsible?"

"Who? God, I guess."

"Not what I mean."

"Diablo?" I said with a little levity.

"Not funny, Mr. Short. I could have been killed."

Callus. "I'm truly sorry, Mrs. Moore, but I have no idea who is responsible."

"Aren't you?"

I was new at this, but everyone had insurance, right? "Don't you have insurance for your belongings?"

"Dios mio! You're my landlord. You must have insurance, verdad?"

"Verdad, Mrs. Moore, for my things, not yours."

"Como?"

"I have insurance, but only for the appliances, carpets, my stuff."

Silence.

"Mrs. Moore, do you understand?"

"So, if your appliances (she struggled with that word) broke down and my food went bad, water gushed all over the place from the toilet, including my things, we'd be covered, no?"

I was beginning to understand through her accent. "Mrs. Moore, how much will it cost to replace your TV?"

Fink was okay with my decision, considering the Moores had been good tenants. He had mentioned we would have to bend the rules at times. We sold the unit, made a few bucks, and that was the end to our real estate partnership. Or so I thought.

Fink called me today, all excited. He was at Miami International waiting for his flight back to New York after signing the contract on his new retirement digs. "To be closer to my retired buddy." He picked a condo with a magnificent view of Biscayne Bay from a photo in the Sunday New York Times real estate section. He believed buying now insured him against price increases. And he loved Key Biscayne. Who didn't?

Key Biscayne, a causeway throw from Miami, had become very expensive, and frankly, a little too hurricane prone for me. But I knew there was no talking him out of it, so I just congratulated him.

"Not me, Eddie. Us. I want us to be partners."

Though gracious, I reminded him I was a newly retired pensioner with no seed money.

Fink said he had enough money for both of us, and he would buy my share at the fair market value when he eventually retired into the unit . . . unless the market declined and I would have to wait for my profit.

There was only one clause in our oral contract that Fink insisted on. As before, I would be responsible for collecting the rent and keeping the property in mint condition. For that, I would enjoy 25 percent ownership.

I couldn't wait to tell Kate I was a real estate mogul.

SPEED BUMPS

Life was littered with speed bumps. You know those setbacks that hit at once without warning. I remembered driving down a two-lane road from Cancun to the Chichen Itza ruins with no air-conditioning under intense sun when I hit a speed bump at 60 mph about halfway through the three hours. I slammed my head into the roof of the car. The ruins took a backseat to my headache, and it still ached the next morning until a Motrin gave me relief. It was a minor setback, like ominous clouds at your child's outdoor birthday party forcing you inside.

Other speed bumps were more complicated, such as canceling a party because of sickness or death. But we handled those too. We had to.

Retirement had its own speed bumps and occurred more rapidly, and with a vengeance, as we approached the top of life's pyramid, those mythical golden years everyone talked about. More bumps with less endurance to handle them.

For younger and healthier retirees with the strength and means to ride out a few more storms, those ominous clouds still blindsided us.

For us, it started off as a typical sunny South Florida morning. Kate was nurturing her plants on the patio, and I was keeping my computer company. The phone rang, and I rolled back my chair to see if Kate heard it. She didn't or pretended not to, and since I was closer, curious and not nurturing anything at the moment, I answered it on the fourth ring.

"Is Mrs. Short home?" a woman asked.

Damn telemarketer. "Who's calling her?" I asked impatiently.

"Is this Mr. Short?"

"Who's calling him?"

Hesitation. "It has to do with Mrs. Wilson."

"Franny?" I asked with sudden interest. "Is she okay?"

"Oh, hi, I'm Mary, her neighbor. I'm afraid she fell down in her apartment this morning. Well, it might have happened last night."

"But is she okay?"

"I'm not sure. Is this Mr. Short?"

"Eddie, yes, please go on."

"Yes, well, I had to call 911 after finding her on the floor."

I scratched my head, trying to envision my elderly mother-in-law in her New York apartment dragging herself to the door. "How did she let you in if she was on the floor?"

Mary hesitated again, then said she had a spare key. "When she didn't answer the door, I opened it. We go out for a walk every morning."

Settle down, Eddie. "Where is she now, Mary?"

"The ambulance took her about an hour ago. . . . She was complaining about her hip yesterday. You think it might be her hip?"

"Certainly sounds like it," I agreed. She is old. "Do you know what hospital they took her to?"

More silence. "I think the paramedics said New Rochelle Medical Center. It's the closest one from here."

My mind was racing.

"Mr. Short?"

"How did you find us? I mean, we're not listed."

"Oh, that. I told you I have a key to Franny's apartment. We exchanged keys just in case. Anyway, I was looking around for her phone book when I came across Kate's name and phone number on the refrigerator door."

"Refrigerator?"

"It was on one of those yellow things."

"Stickys. That was smart."

Mary said she wondered whether Franny had a premonition because she hadn't noticed the Sticky before. Believe me, my mother-in-law never thought in those terms. She was too independent to imagine a sore hip slowing her down.

Mary must have been starved for conversation because now she was gabbing about her cat, Whiskers. Given that she was nice enough to call, I tolerated a few minutes while watching Kate interact with her plants as though she hadn't a care in the world. When Mary stopped for air, I said, "Thanks for calling. I better tell Kate."

"Of course. Doesn't Franny have another daughter?"

"Laura. Why do you ask?"

"It's just that only Kate's number was on the refrigerator."

I assumed Franny hadn't discussed her family history with her walking partner or Whiskers, and I wasn't about to break the seal. "Must have been an oversight. Is there a number I can reach you at, Mary, just in case?"

Mary rattled off her phone number. "Call me anytime."

"You're a good neighbor, Mary. Franny speaks of you frequently," I lied.

"We're very close. She was there for me when my husband died."

Obviously, not close enough to know the sordid details about Laura. I was beginning to glean how the elderly support system worked. Who would be there for Kate? Or me? Who would knock on our door and find one of us sprawled out like a crime scene victim? I made a mental note to post Jesse's number on our fridge.

How was this going to play out with Kate's older sister? My mother-in-law hadn't forgotten to add Laura's phone number in case of an emergency; their relationship had been strained for years. I could only imagine Laura's misplaced anger at Kate had she discovered the 'Stickys' plot.

Kate must have been in deep thought watering her crown of thorns because she didn't notice me approaching.

"Hey," I said tenderly.

She blinked, smiled, then caught my somber expression. "Everything okay?"

There was no easy way to break it. "Apparently, your mother fell in her apartment." I squeezed her shoulder. "Her neighbor, Mary, just called."

Kate recoiled. "Is she all right? Where is she? . . . "

I couldn't keep up with her questions. "Slow down, Kate. It was just a fall."

Kate handed me the watering can and bolted for the door. "I have to go to her!"

I followed her inside. "Kate, there's nothing you can do until I find you a flight."

She slumped in a chair. "Does Laura know?"

I shrugged. "Mary didn't say." I didn't mention the Sticky on the refrigerator.

"I better call her," she said, getting up.

"How about I call?" I knew Kate's anxiety escalated every time they spoke.

"Would you mind, Eddie?" Her eyes were begging.

I nodded and waited until Kate returned to her flowers. Laura lived in Los Angeles, so the three-hour time difference meant she probably was putting the finishing touches on her face.

"Hey, Laura, it's Eddie," I said, sounding cheery.

Laura didn't respond, so I wondered whether we got disconnected. But it must have finally registered because concern laced her voice when she asked, "Eddie, is everything okay?"

"Mom had a slight fall, so we thought you ought to know. Nothing serious."

"Slight fall?"

I didn't want to panic her. After all, she was still blood. A friend once told me about his faux pas in calling his sister about a cat he was watching for her.

"Tipsy fell off the roof and died," he had blurted out. She had admonished him for being insensitive. He obviously wasn't a pet owner, or he would have relayed the message a bit different, such as, "Tipsy fell off the roof and hurt a leg, so I rushed her to the vet where they performed surgery gallantly, but unfortunately, there were complications. Sis, Tipsy passed peacefully. I'm so sorry." He wised up the next time when his sister couldn't reach their mother after returning from another trip.

"Mom fell off the roof, Laura," wouldn't work, so I said, "I'm not sure how bad the fall was. The doctors are with her now."

"You're in New York?"

"No, her neighbor called." Get it right, Eddie. "Apparently, the woman kept our phone number from our Christmas card last year." Another Pinocchio. "Mom is at the New Rochelle Medical Center. I'm trying to get Kate a flight for this afternoon."

"Is she there?" Laura asked tentatively.

I peered outside. "She's taking a shower and asked me to call you." I was getting good at this.

"I appreciate the call, Eddie," she said stiffly. "How is Kate taking it?"

"She's upset, as you can imagine. Your mother is a strong eight-five-year old, so I'm sure she'll mend in no time."

"Hope so."

Franny was a spry senior who still played tennis twice a week, drove, and had a boyfriend who recently passed away after a night on the town. Who knew what on the town meant at that age?

"I better call my office and tell them I'll be away for a while."

Laura retired last year at sixty-five but couldn't take the sedentary life, so she worked part time at a charity gift shop. She hadn't been in a serious relationship since divorcing Billy, who, according to Laura, was one partner too many for a lifetime.

"Thanks. I'm sure Kate will appreciate the support."

Laura was silent a moment, then said Kate was lucky to have me and she would try to catch a flight this afternoon too.

I jumped online and found a JetBlue flight to JFK, which wasn't cheap, considering it was last minute. Where was Billy when I needed him? Which reminded me, I needed to break the news to him. He still exchanged Christmas cards with Franny.

I smelled Kate's ambrosial perfume at my back. "She take it okay?"

I nodded and pressed enter to finalize my transaction. "Got you on a four o'clock flight. You'll be at the hospital by eight tonight."

"Thanks. . . . She say anything?"

I could tell Kate had been crying. I took her hand. "Laura is looking to fly in tonight. Maybe you'll arrive about the same time?" That probably wasn't the right thing to say, given Kate's upper lip stiffening. "You'll be fine. Would you feel better if I found you a hotel?"

She shook her head. "I have to deal with her. I'll stay at Mom's place."

I shrugged. "Who knows, maybe you guys will come to an understanding?"

She looked at the floor. "She's still angry at me for getting most of Mom's affection over the years. I'm not about to bring up the issue."

"I'm sure Laura will when she's ready. This might be that time."

Kate feigned a smile. "She wasn't when Dad died."

"Laura is older now. This fall might motivate her into realizing that time is short."

Kate smiled wistfully. "Want to be a referee?"

HALF A SANDWICH – HOLD THE PICKLE

With eight months into retirement, Kate and I were the newest members of what I called the half sandwich generation, not to be confused with the sandwich generation, which sounded more like a culinary club destined to enhance the mundane BLT. Instead, the sandwich generation was about 25 percent of Americans who were squeezed between their children and aging parents who needed assistance.

The nationally syndicated newspaper columnist, Carol Abaya, a recognized expert on the sandwich generation, coined two additional groups. The first, the club sandwich consisting of people in their fifties and sixties sandwiched between aging parents, adult children, and grandchildren; or, those in their thirties and forties with young children, aging parents, and grandparents. And the second, the open face sandwich, threw in everyone else involved in elder care. Kate and I didn't quite fit into the above scenarios since

Jesse lived alone and was no longer our responsibility, and while technically speaking, we were in the open face camp, I much rather considered myself a half sandwich. Once my mother-in-law returned home, I would renew my membership in the do-nothing generation.

Kate's mother survived her hip fracture, thanks in part to her walking partner. Franny apparently tripped over the TV remote that morning and tumbled onto the carpet. She didn't own one of those I-fell-down-and-can't-get-up monitors, which she claimed were for old people, so she had to wait for Mary to save the day.

The fall itself wasn't the problem; Franny suffered from osteoporosis and apparently was at risk for fractures. We couldn't blame the innocuous remote, could we? The surgery went well, thanks to Franny's health, and with additional therapy in Florida, was on her way home in no time.

Those thoughts occupied my time while waiting for Kate and Franny at Palm Beach International three weeks after the incident. Franny's fall might have been a blessing for Kate and Laura, who had little choice but to face their sibling issues while staying at their mother's apartment. At first, Laura was reserved and distant, and it didn't help when Laura found Kate and her mother holding hands at the hospital. Deep wounds.

But an uncomfortable silence turned into a catharsis with yelling and name-calling, followed by crying and hugs. The first peeling of the onion continued the second night. By the time Laura left for L.A., her misplaced anger toward Kate began to dissipate as she recognized the real culprit: Franny. My mother-in-law found it difficult to admit fault, and I suspected Laura never would resolve her issues with Franny. But throughout her stay, Laura proved to be the compassionate and dutiful daughter.

Of course, Kate related all this to me and thanked me for pushing her to reconnect. She was ecstatic. The sisters promised to call, e-mail, and visit on a regular basis. I hoped it wasn't just wishful thinking.

I'd always gotten along with my mother-in-law, the independent soul she was. Franny never meddled in our lives. But outside of the guest bedroom, our townhouse afforded little privacy.

I spotted Kate pushing Franny in a wheelchair from the terminal. The weight of the trip etched her face. And I was a bit shocked at how frail Franny looked, not the usual robust woman. She appeared confused until Kate pointed me out. Franny waved a limp arm and smiled—a sad, almost resigned smile. I gave her a tender hug and kissed her forehead as I watched a thin smile bud on Kate's weary face.

"How about a round of golf, Franny?" Kate scowled, but Franny said, "I forgot my clubs, Eddie. Sorry." At least she still had a sense of humor, though her voice was barely above a whisper.

"It's too hot anyway," I said.

Kate stopped the wheelchair near the baggage claim area and told her mother to stick around until she returned. Like she had a choice.

"My mother is depressed, Eddie," Kate said softly as she searched the conveyor belt before turning to me. "She didn't want to leave her apartment and friends."

"Who could blame her? She's very independent."

She bit her lower lip. "This is going to kill her."

I glanced at Franny, who was staring into space. "She on painkillers?"

Kate nodded. "The doctor feels she should be on antidepressants too, but my stubborn mother refuses. All she's ever taken were vitamins."

"She's been lucky up to now."

Kate waved at her mother. "She's definitely not herself, Eddie. When I tell her she'll be walking in no time, she cries like a baby."

"I thought the operation went well."

"It did."

My eyes studied Kate's. "You're not telling me everything, are you?"

Kate pointed at a suitcase with a red string on the handle. "That's ours."

I scooped up my mother-in-law's suitcase, nearly snapping my back. "What the hell is in here? Her apartment?"

"She forgets."

I dropped the suitcase. “Who doesn’t?”

“A lot. Laura noticed it too. Her apartment was a mess, everything out of place. And you know how meticulous my mother is.”

I stared at Franny’s suitcase. “This isn’t temporary, is it?”

Kate pointed at another suitcase being dumped onto the conveyor belt. “I didn’t want to tell you until I got home.”

Another red string attached to the handle. I wasn’t about to be too aggressive snatching this one. “I smell a road trip coming.”

Kate closed her eyes. “She can’t live alone, Eddie. Not now.”

“Or ever, apparently.”

“The doctor says she shouldn’t be alone.”

I stole a glance at Franny, then back at Kate. “They have assisted living facilities—”

“That’s out of the question!”

Wow, she was at a breaking point. “Maybe you and Laura can take turns watching her . . . .” What was I thinking?

“She can’t take care of Mom.”

“Can’t or won’t?”

“She has only one bedroom. Eddie, please don’t be difficult.”

“You’re right, Kate. I’m sorry. It won’t be a problem.”

She produced a wistful smile and touched my arm. “Thanks for understanding.”

“Any more suitcases?” I touched my lower back.

“Only mine.”

One big happy family. I schlepped the suitcases toward my mother-in-law, who appeared to be finding space interesting. My cell went off. Oh good, time to rest. It was Jesse. I listened, occasionally nodded, then hung up and joined Franny staring into space. I smelled a club sandwich coming on.

WHEN IT RAINS IT POURS

One big happy family. Did I mention that already? That was before Jesse broached the news of his breakup with Rebecca, who he'd been living with for the past three years. She was a great woman: smart, charming, and beautiful, with an exciting job that demanded extensive traveling. There lay the problem. Rebecca was on her way to becoming director of international operations for a major public relations firm. Unfortunately, Jesse was standing in her way. It's not like he didn't want Rebecca to pursue her goal, but he wanted to get married and start a family. Only right now, Rebecca's company was her family. With no compromise in sight, Jesse moved out.

As a parent, I felt his pain. As a man, I wanted to fix it. But all I could do was listen, hold his hand, and remind him that mi casa es su casa. So at thirty-three, Jesse reluctantly moved back with us—temporarily. Kate was all smiles, but Jesse felt humiliated, a failure. I certainly understood and assured him he'd eventually find someone to share his life with in time.

Jesse needed to find an apartment. Our tiny townhouse already was cramped with Franny, which relegated Jesse to my cave. So I had to wait until Jesse left for work before I could hop onto my computer, a minor inconvenience as a retiree. And this was temporary, right?

Three generations under one roof was a novelty, and I was quite fine with it. For the first time since the pilgrims, we passed bread around the dinner table. Kate had been searching her cookbooks for exotic recipes, some I couldn't even pronounce. At dinner, we'd discuss everything from movies to world events, with Franny occasionally keeping up. After dinner, Jesse helped with the dishes while Franny and I fought over the remote, though I made sure it didn't land on the floor. One hip fracture was enough.

We lived in a transient society with family members moving away for job opportunities, better retirement settings, or escaping bad relationships. Ironically, we were closer than ever to our loved ones, thanks to the Internet. Yet, did we really know what was behind the cloak of an e-mail? No wonder Franny's slow mental changes went undetected until her fall. Distance created limitations on family gatherings. Even phone calls, texts, or Facebook didn't always reveal transparencies.

That's what happened with Franny, and no one was to blame, especially Kate. She was a good daughter, always keeping in touch, asking her mother if she needed anything. But Franny had her own life twelve hundred miles away. Who wouldn't have thought Franny's dementia wasn't just some old age thing?

Change had entered the Short household as we divided our time between doctors and cooking, though Franny ate very little anymore. We stayed home more, turning to videos and board games. Jesse, a homebody, was great with his grandmother, pushing her mentally with cards and Jeopardy. It made me love him even more. He was a wonderful grandson who would remember his grandmother's final days and hopefully appreciate his own life.

Franny's debilitating Alzheimer's disease fell between the early and middle stages. She became more forgetful—even more than me—of details and recent events. She'd repeat herself and sometimes stop in the middle of a conversation, lost and frustrated. As a result, she'd become irritable and angry.

A few weeks into Franny's stay with us—definitely not a visit—Kate and I decided I should take a road trip to clean out Franny's apartment. We spared Franny the experience of moving day; it would have devastated her to watch us clean out her past.

We found snippets of her recent life: old newspapers, reams of plastic supermarket bags, and unopened cereal boxes in her bedroom closet. Jesse accompanied me on the road trip; he wanted a diversion from his breakup from Rebecca, and I needed a strong back. Kate had given me a list of items to bring back, including all photos, Franny's Mikasa china, and anything that looked antique. Sorry, Laura, we were here first.

Franny's kitchen table provided more evidence of confusion and forgetfulness. That's where I found a pile of unpaid bills sitting on top of her checkbook, along with threatening reminders from creditors. I immediately paid them. I also discovered my mother-in-law spent more money at department stores than Kate. Finally, I read a notice from the New York State Department of Motor Vehicles, wincing at the thought of Franny renewing her license. Further examination revealed she had gotten into a fender bender at the supermarket and took off without exchanging licenses. The other driver must have called the police, who paid Franny a visit. Franny, of course, never mentioned the incident to Kate, and maybe didn't even remember it. But the bottom line? Franny was issued a citation for leaving the scene. At some point, she would have been required to take a driver safety reexamination interview. That was moot now, of course. Good-bye, license.

I paid Mary a visit and realized why she never contacted us about Franny's mental state. She too repeated things and talked about her past as though it were yesterday. With no family outside of Whiskers, what was in store for her? I thanked Mary again for calling us and invited her to pick out a few tchotchkes at Franny's apartment. She loved the blue ceramic teapot.

The final unpleasant experience was selling Franny's car, the last vestige of her independent living. I checked with the building superintendent, a nice guy from Bosnia or Montenegro, I can't remember, and explained my situation. His eyes lit up when I offered a good price. Sold!

From the beginning, Kate swore off nursing homes, that her mother never would live with strangers. But at some point, Franny's bad days would outnumber the good ones, when she would ramble more with vacant eyes, when Kate had to dress and bathe her. By then, support groups would play a major role in our lives.

You would think Franny's doomsday situation was imminent by the stress Kate was assuming, talking incessantly about Franny going from independent to dependent to Depends someday. She always had been overprotective, which I believed made Franny more frustrated. As for my sex life, that too was in transition; I usually got lucky when Franny had a good day. But I understood and was patient.

Fortunately, retirement meant reporting to no one, but I felt our window of independence and opportunity narrowing. Time we had assumed was guaranteed like a gold watch was ticking away too quickly. Right now, our future was in Franny's hands.

WHO'S WATCHING YOUR LIFE?

Kate accused me of being obsessed with the mail. And mailboxes. Over the years, our mailbox had been shaped like animals, cars, and a New England cedar house, to Kate's chagrin. I loved New England. Kate believed it was part of my infantile humor. The mail carriers seemed to like them, but maybe they were humoring me.

I admit the first thing I did when I arrived home from work was to grab my daily trove from Elvis the Hound Dog or the Pink Cadillac. I'd categorize the mail into three piles: bills, potential, and junk. I'd open junk mail first to build excitement for the real stuff. I tossed the junk into the garbage unless it piqued my curiosity. On to the bills. I'd note the payment dates on the envelopes, then stack them in a basket on my desk in chronological order. That was the anal accountant in me.

The potential category felt like holding a long-shot ticket, hoping the state was informing me that my crazy uncle left me a million dollars. If only I had a crazy uncle . . .

For certain, I didn't enjoy getting other people's mail, nor did I want some Joe Blow knowing my business, especially if it was the state informing me the million dollars from Uncle Joey's estate would stay with the state if I didn't act quickly.

Face it, most mail was worthless. It was that one nugget—a store rebate or a birthday card with cash—that teased with a little suspense. Or, that letter from the finance company congratulating you for paying off your car loan. Hurray, no more late charges!

I obviously wasn't racing home from work anymore, but I frequently waited outside for our carrier's usual time, the loyal customer I was.

Today was no exception. I stood underneath an umbrella next to our metal calico cat, Boo Boo, keeping us both dry. Like clockwork, Jeannie arrived and looked great—as in a killer makeover, dressed to the nines in a black taffeta dress. And in a downpour in a mail truck! We chatted about her weekly night out with her husband, Dan. Tonight, they were topping an early dinner with the theater. Jeannie didn't want to keep Dan waiting, so she waved good-bye after showing me a new photograph of her grandchild.

Inside the house, I felt cheated on the lean delivery: no junk, bills from Macy's and Bloomingdale's (meaning Kate's window shopping turned irresistible), and a letter from my life insurance company, which I assumed was informing me that my dividends were growing and my cash value had increased significantly over last year.

But it didn't read that way. Instead, it decreed I would have to surrender my policy if I didn't start forking over a much higher premium. Perplexed, I forgot about protocol, tossed the bills on the kitchen table, and entered my cave. I read all serious documents in this room because it created an environment of self-importance, a place to make tough decisions like when I worked.

Being a numbers guy, I knew when they didn't add up, and this statement didn't make sense. I reread it and compared figures from last year, praying for a mistake. I never would have considered a life insurance policy that would force me to surrender it because of outlandish premiums. My agent knew that. In fact, he assured me my premiums would remain the same, decrease, or possibly cease.

I tapped my nails on the desk in a frenzied cadence. This was potentially devastating. It could change my financial security, or rather Kate's, at a time when she needed it the most.

I started working for the federal government when pensions were fixed, meaning my monthly check was set regardless of whether the stock market, real estate market, or any other market crashed in front of me. My pension also offered an option: a survivor benefit, which provided a lesser amount to my beneficiary. Of course, that benefit came with a premium, which was subtracted from my monthly pension check. Fair enough. Less money today meant an annuity for Kate later. Once Kate left this Earth, assuming after me, the pension stopped. Sorry, Jesse.

As a taxman, I knew that replacing the survivor benefit with the right life insurance policy not only provided tax free monetary comfort to my first beneficiary, but also Kate would provide a tidy sum to my secondary beneficiary, Jesse, assuming she didn't spend it like a drunken sailor. And so, with my agent's blessing, I opted for life insurance over the survivor benefit.

If this annual report was correct, it would change my estate planning because I could wind up paying twenty thousand in the near future instead of seven thousand a year in premiums. Poor Kate and Jesse. We were screwed!

My hands shook as I dialed Murray, my insurance guy. As usual, he didn't answer, so I left a detailed message. I paced about in my socks and shined the Pergo floors until it hit me. A few months back, Murray had called touting an incredibly rewarding life policy with plenty of bells and whistles, some type of indexed universal life policy tied to the stock market. Like I said, I'm a numbers guy, but nobody can work numbers like insurance companies. The average person didn't understand the intricacies of insurance policies, including some agents, so clients relied on professionals to get through the maze of—numbers.

Satisfied with my existing policy, I thanked Murray for the offer, but bells and whistles were for younger guys, especially since I had been paying premiums for six years and didn't want to restart the fees and commissions. Besides, exotic policies came with exotic commissions. I only could imagine how much of my new premium might pay for Murray's next exotic vacation.

I was about to head to the bathroom when the phone rang. It was Murray, who must have sensed my panic. Murray Wilson had been an independent agent for more than twenty years, had a wife and two great kids, like that guy buying term insurance in one of those TV commercials. He lived in a McMansion, drove a top-of-the-line BMW 7 Series, and decorated his conference room with photos from his latest vacation. Last year, the family went to Maui, rather mundane from the previous year to Fiji.

"Hey, Eddie, what's new?"

He obviously hadn't listened to my message, or was an insensitive idiot. "I need to see you immediately."

"Gee, Eddie, I have a client coming in shortly—"

"There's something terribly wrong with my annual report. I need to see you now!"

I knew Murray also had received my report because of the cc to him at the bottom of the insurance company's letter. And his silence told me he had read it.

He coughed. "Can it wait until tomorrow, Eddie? I'll have time then."

"Not if you want to attend my funeral."

"Eddie, take it easy. I reviewed your report this morning. I admit we need to discuss it, but nothing is going to change in twenty-four hours."

I squeezed my knees together as my bladder crested. "You don't understand, Murray. Kate's financial future is riding on this. I can't wait twenty-four hours. How long will you need with your client?"

"About an hour I guess, but—"

"See you in an hour." I hung up and raced for the bathroom, but this time I didn't get the usual satisfaction. I zipped up, grabbed my insurance file, and dashed out the door.

I-95 was a wet mess as my Civic snaked through blinding rain. Thank God Kate wasn't around to hear me swear. Which reminded me, she didn't have a clue where I was going. Then again, I didn't know where she was. Probably scouting sales at Macy's or Bloomies. I'd call her later.

By the time I reached Murray's office, my mind was spinning. For the past hour, I'd been envisioning Kate swearing at my gravesite for screwing up again, instead of crying sweet tears.

Drenched, I stormed into Murray's office, where the secretary asked if I would like a towel and coffee.

"Only Murray." I scowled, displacing my displeasure on her.

"I'll tell him you're here, Mr. Short." She disappeared into the next room.

Murray's latest client appeared first, a guy about my age who nodded as he passed. Unlike me, "I'm Screwed" wasn't scrawled on his forehead.

Murray approached and extended his hand. "Eddie, you got wet."

He obviously had been too busy earning his next vacation to notice the weather. I obliged a quick shake, his hand a dead fish. "Let's talk."

He ushered me into his conference room. "I think we have a problem," he finally said.

We? How about me?

Murray picked up my report and studied it as though it were the first time. "I think the company was too hopeful with their numbers."

"You mean unrealistic." I plopped my wet ass in his leather chair.

He hesitated before sitting behind his desk. "Maybe. Yeah, possibly."

I nodded a few times as water from my hair landed on his desk. "Well, it's a good thing I brought this problem to your attention. Now you can alert your other clients about this … what is it again?"

He cleared his throat. "Graded premium whole life."

"Right. The kind where the premium isn't set for the life of the policy."

Murray coughed as though he was about to expel more bad news. "There's been scuttlebutt." He averted his eyes. "Apparently, when the company introduced the policy, they thought it would pay higher dividends to its policyholders." He glanced up and attempted to smile.

"It's pretty obvious from the report that they thought of themselves first."

Murray cleared his throat again before more venom escaped. "They obviously miscalculated, Eddie."

I focused on Murray's vacation glossies and shook my head. "You said scuttlebutt. So you and the other agents saw this coming? . . . When were you going to tell me?"

Murray hesitated before manipulating a maze of nonsense, advising me the premiums technically could call for an increase. He shuffled through his file for a form with my signature, like it was his defense.

My hands gripped the side of his desk as my voice rose. "You knew I was going to retire on a fixed income. You knew I never would be able to afford another $14,000 a year. Yet, you got me into this, this piece of shit!"

Murray's face turned red. "I'm sorry, Eddie. I really thought-"

"You didn't think."

Murray's Adam's apple bobbled. "Eddie, I can try to get you into that other policy we spoke about recently." He didn't even mention it by name.

I pointed at his chest. “You mean that exotic indexing policy?”

He nodded rapidly. “Index, right. You can sign a release form so we can get started with a physical. Okay?”

I shook my head slowly. “Not OK, Murray, but what choice do I have? And by the way, I might not be insurable anymore.”

Murray stiffened. “Why not?”

“I recently was diagnosed with sleep apnea.”

Murray, who never was short on words, remained silent.

I leaned across his desk. “Here’s the rub, Mr. Reliable Insurance Man. I can’t get back into the government survivor benefit plan because it’s beyond the eighteen-month grace period. I’m fucked!”

Murray flinched. I never swore at Murray before, but I wanted him to understand how screwed I was.

“Shit.” He exhaled and fixed his eyes on the wall behind me.

“So where do we go from here?” I finally asked.

He turned to me. “You’re sure about this?”

“Oh yeah.”

He dropped his head in his hands. “I’ll think of something, Eddie, I swear.” Murray was a natural salesman.

“The way I see it, I have three choices.”

Murray lifted his head. “Please.”

“First, I can buy a gun and blow away everyone who’s responsible for this mess. Only that would require doing time, and the prison food might kill me.”

Murray raised a hand. "Eddie, please don't talk like that."

"Two, I can jump in front of a subway car. That way, the insurance company will be forced to pay Kate the full amount. Only I love New York too much to make a mess of myself there."

"This is not funny."

"Or, I can go to the *Federal Times*, *AARP*, and any other interested party willing to expose the industry and its agents. If nothing else, it will make people aware of these policies." I paused with a sinister smile. "You might want to let the insurance company know my intentions."

My trusted agent blanched.

Driving home, I called Kate, who was window-shopping at The Gardens Mall in Palm Beach Gardens. Where else? She asked about my day, but I knew there weren't enough cell plan minutes to last through my saga. She told me I was in for a treat from Victoria's Secret.

Just what I needed! At home, I grabbed a Michelob Ultra from the fridge. Ninety calories, though my thoughts weren't on weight loss. Would Murray and the insurance company ameliorate the situation or call my bluff? I was just screwed.

I downed the beer and reached for another, then another, trying to get in the mood before Kate got home.

HELP THY CHEAP FRIENDS

It had been about a month after Franny and Jesse joined the Short household. Jesse regrouped and started meeting friends for dinner while Franny cried about his absence and mostly holed up in her room watching TV. Kate attempted to divert her attention by taking her to the mall or to lunch by the beach. That left me alone and dangerous.

Before leaving to get their hair done, my passive-aggressive wife asked me to research everything I could find on Alzheimer's: what to expect, what to fear, medical breakthroughs, and support groups. Kate never had a yen for surfing the Web, arguing it was a time suck from more productive things. I hated when she disparaged my interests.

I was about to leave the official Alzheimer's site when an instant message popped up on my screen. I didn't recognize the name, so I didn't respond. But the writer persisted with another message, "HOW'S RETIREMENT?" That piqued my curiosity, so I wrote back, "Great, how's life treating you?"

"You don't know who this is, do you?" shot across my screen.

Busted. "OF COURSE, I DO." I checked my contact names and discovered it was Wallace Jones II from the Manhattan IRS office. I hadn't heard from him since he apologized for missing my luncheon, not that I expected him to catch a flight to Fort Lauderdale. To make up for it, he offered to buy me lunch if I ever made it to New York. Knowing Wallace, we'd wind up at a deli for tuna on rye.

I knew Wallace had been contemplating retirement lately and he'd finally hit the wall, though he'd been tossing around the R word on his anniversary for the past four years.

"How's life, Wallace?" I typed.

"I hate this job, Eddie. I'm broad and hate my buss," he wrote, obviously too lazy to use spell-check. "You're great at helping people. What do you think I should do???"

Wallace was ingratiating me because it didn't cost him anything. It was like using a gift card every time he wanted something, only I wasn't in the mood to listen to the same old discussion. "Retire already!"

"You sure?"

How long had Wallace been skulking around waiting to IM me? God knows, he'd never pick up the phone. You had to understand Wallace, close to sixty, never married, and didn't have kids unless his condom broke on R&R in Thailand. Rumor had it that his savings account balance included money from his first paycheck, so he wasn't financially impaired. But Wallace worried about money and believed he never would save enough. Sounded a little like Fink, but believe me, Wallace was no Fink. If you were familiar with Wallace's lifestyle, however, you'd probably agree with him. He rented a modest apartment and drove the smallest stick-shift car ever made, which he boasted got umpteen miles per gallon. Wallace always drove in the slow lane and never inched the accelerator beyond the speed limit. With today's gas prices, I admit it made sense.

Wallace must have been surprised by my terse answer, but like I said, I wasn't in the mood. However, again, he persisted and fired back his litany of reasons why he should retire, which I'd heard before. This time, though, he threw in a curve ball: Wallace Jones II was in love.

"Good for you," I wrote back, resisting the urge to add, "I'm shocked." Did I mention he hated to spend money?

"She's a great gal! We have so much in common."

Like the same driving habits? "Young, old? How'd you meet?" I hammered out every other question I could type in a minute.

"We met online. I used my buddy's password."

Naturally. "Meet her in the flesh yet?"

"At the local library."

That's my Wallace, no bar bills. "She must love to read."

"Not really, it was conveennt for both of us."

Spell-check, please! "Makes sense."

"She's like me, lives a simple life."

That was overstating it. Wallace's pre-war apartment building sat above the subway system, so he was less than thirty minutes to the office. Since moving into his rent-control one bedroom thirty years ago, his rent was less than my mortgage. And I didn't have one!

"She lives only two subway stops away."

"Lucky you. Kids?"

"Never married."

As I mentioned, Wallace had never married either, so I gave him a "Smart" with an underline.

"She's had relationships over the years but never met Mr. Right until now." Most of Wallace's relationships had been with Washington and Lincoln. "We're pretty serious even though it's only been a month."

At our age, a month was a lifetime. "Do I hear wedding bells?"

A good minute passed before, "Maybe. That's why I contacted you. You're the guy with all the answers."

Did I mention Wallace was a taker?

"It's about a financial arrangement."

"A PRENUP IS IMPERATIVE," I wrote.

"She wouldn't have it any other way."

"Smart."

"She's pretty well off, probably still has money from her first paycheck as a teacher. Ha ha."

We were so blinded by ourselves.

"Not that I need her money, mind you. It's just that if we're considering marriage, I feel a prenup is an impediment. You know, breeds failure."

"So you're okay with possibly giving up half of yours if you end up in a divorce?" I was so cruel.

"Hell, no!!" came back quickly.

Guessed he got my point.

"I suppose she's right," Wallace wrote.

"Believe me, she's right."

"So you're okay with it?"

Considering I wouldn't lose a dime, I was fine with it. "Makes sense to me. She'll feel better about the relationship, and so will you. That way, it can't get too messy if the marriage doesn't work out. . . . BUT I'M SURE IT WILL WORK!!" I added as a wedding gift.

"Thanks, Eddie. I knew I could rely on you. Ever consider becoming a life coach for pre-retirees?"

That was an idea Kate would embrace. "Thanks for the compliment. Something to consider." I asked Wallace about his dating arrangements.

"We usually meet somewhere in the middle, take turns paying for dinner or a movie, then go back to her place where I spend the night."

Her place must be cleaner. "The sex good?"

"That's personal, Eddie!!"

I was about to mention that sex was a standard life coach issue, but typed, "I'm just asking because it's an important part of a relationship."

"Oh, okay. It's pretty good."

Pretty good? He should be on fire only a month in!

Then he wrote, "We have a lot of things in common."

Sex must be bad. "Sounds like I'll be getting an invitation."

A delay. "It's going to be very small."

Rejected again.

"Justice of the peace."

"No fanfare, huh? Even though it's the first for both of you?"

"We talked it over and prefer to spend our money on a honeymoon. Maybe drive out West."

A right lane road trip. "Of course."

"You would have been on my list, Eddie."

"Appreciate it, Wallace. Best of luck to both of you. Chat with you another time."

I was about to sign off when "Wait!!!" flashed up. "What about retirement?"

I could have recommended he retire before his future mother-in-law got sick and moved in, but I'd given enough free advice for one day.

"Someone's at my door," I typed.

HELLO COLONOSCOPY

Franny's dementia got me thinking: How many more summers did I have on this Earth? My family doctor once told me sixty-five was the crossover age into accelerated mortality. In histrionic fashion, he cautioned we could die from sickness, get hit by a bus or a hit man before receiving full social security, but our genes dominated in the long run. Unfortunately, my tribe didn't offer much insight. My father died from cirrhosis of the liver at fifty—well, technically a heart attack, and my mother, who died on her seventieth birthday from a hit-and-run accident while walking across a busy street to retrieve a Vote Here sign after her candidate won the election, complained about every ailment known to man in retirement.

The only other relatives in my gene pool were my mother's brother, the loser Uncle Willie, who believed in long shots. Poor Willie died under mysterious circumstances at thirty-five. In arrears with an impatient loan shark, my uncle suffered broken legs that left him crippled. Six months later, Uncle Willie was killed by an oncoming car, probably driven by the same guy who realized my uncle's disability checks wouldn't cover his exorbitant interest rate due to his bookie, much less his loan.

Then there was my father's sister, Dolores, who died of malaria in her twenties while on a mission—a real mission with missionaries helping the sick in Brazil's rainforest. My father, guilt-ridden for suggesting she leave a comfortable lifestyle for good causes, started drinking soon after. That and the horrors he witnessed as a medic in Tarawa sent him into an abyss.

So my family's legacy, outside of my mother's hypochondria, stopped short of the sixty-five threshold. To counter that, I didn't smoke, I consumed assorted vitamins daily, and exercised by taking out the garbage. Kate had been after me for years to get a colonoscopy, but I refused until I began witnessing sickness, death, and especially my mother-in-law's fall and dementia. Say hello, colonoscopy.

My family doctor referred me to a gastroenterologist, a specialist who searched colons for suspicious polyps, sometimes caused by years of old food lining the intestines. In the waiting room, I read a pamphlet on the procedure. The long and short of it—sorry, couldn't resist—explained how the minimally invasive examination of the rectum and colon required a thin, flexible tube to pass through the anus, providing a visual diagnosis of possible ulcerations or polyps, which the doctor could biopsy or remove. Great bathroom reading!

I glanced around at my fellow patients, the majority at least my age. The veterans were stretched out in their seats asleep or watching reruns on TV while the younger, anxious ones probably were braving their first invasion. Unlike me, they were smarter. I was years behind schedule. The American Cancer Society recommended a first screening at fifty unless there was a history of colon cancer in the family, which then dropped the age to forty. Quite frankly, I was too macho at fifty. Or, was it fear? Whatever the reason, my hubris changed as my life began to cross over into the unknown.

Dr. Stevenson greeted me with enthusiasm and pumped my hand with a smile that suggested he enjoyed sticking tubes up his patients' asses. A sadist or just one friendly guy. After a few minutes of heart-to-heart about colon-to-colon, I realized he was the latter who felt rewarded by providing his patients with a clean bill of health.

Dr. Stevenson was about my age with lots of gray hair that Kate would call distinguished looking. He was a people person with seemingly great bedside manners who also performed procedures such as upper gastrointestinal endoscopes and anal hemorrhoidectomies. Very appealing.

After a quick checkup for hemorrhoids, which I didn't have, he assured me the procedure would take about twenty minutes "soup to nuts" (just an expression). He handed me a list of purging aids for preparation and asked if I had any questions.

"Just one: Will it hurt afterward? You know, when I have to go?"

He nodded seriously. "That's a good question, Eddie. The truth is you probably won't be able to sit down for a week."

He watched my face drop, then placed his hand on my shoulder with a broad smile. "Just kidding. You'll be fine. If I have to snip out a polyp for biopsy, you'll never know it. And if I don't find anything suspicious, you won't have to return for five years."

"I'll ask my wife to light a candle. She likes lighting candles."

He nodded. "Good idea. Ask her to light one for me." I searched his face, and he winked. "Piece of cake. . . . You like pancakes, Eddie?"

"Who doesn't?"

"Good. You'll be ready for pancakes soon after the procedure. Ask my receptionist to give you a two-for-one coupon to the Pancake Place across the street. They make great chocolate pancakes."

I liked this guy. On the way home, I stopped off at a drugstore and purchased the preparation items. Simple enough.

The day before my procedure, I consumed enough lunch to carry me through the winter. It had been years since I fasted for more than ten hours.

By two o'clock, I started the purging process. Why did the Fleet enemas require refrigeration? Kate, who was more familiar with this stuff, was out buying shoes with her mother. I swear Franny was faking her disease so she could consume all of Kate's day. Just when I needed her.

By four o'clock, I inserted one of the cold enemas with a tube, but the damn thing froze my insides. I removed it quickly and stared at it. There had to be an easier way. With no one around to suggest otherwise, I decided to wait for the enema to warm up. Fifteen minutes later, I tried to insert the tube slowly in a fetal position, again, and again. "Where the hell is the connection?" I swore, frustrated Kate still wasn't there.

When I gave it one last try, it somehow found its way in. I squeezed the enema and held on until I couldn't take it any longer. Water dripped all over the floor as I leaped up onto the bowl. This was crazy!

For the rest of the afternoon and early evening, I sucked down broth, JELL-O, and water. Kate called to tell me they decided to hit a new sports bar and asked I needed anything.

"A cheeseburger with fries."

"You'll have to wait until after the procedure," Kate said seriously.

"Then why are you asking?"

"Testy, aren't we, Eddie?"

I reminded my wife that while she was out enjoying a few beers, I was stuck at home— just me and my frosty enema.

She started whispering. "I figured with Mom with us, you would rather be alone for the preparation."

"I gotta go."

"Fine, be like that."

"No, I really have to go!"

For the next hour, I sat on the bowl doing the Jumble, reading the comics and every section of the *Post*, even down to the classifieds.

Kate and Franny arrived home all smiles, and Franny asked about my day.

"Did a lot of reading," I said, exhausted.

"You look drained, Eddie."

By 6:00 a.m., my eyes shifted from the clock to the ceiling after being up for hours on the bowl. I woke Kate and reminded her about the pancake breakfast after the procedure. At that point, I would have given away my son for a cookie, but even water was out of the question.

Franny was still asleep when we left at 6:45 a.m.

"I left Mom a note," Kate said. "I hope she finds it on the kitchen table."

"She'll be fine. She's really not that bad off."

She nodded, but not convincingly.

At the surgical center, a tired-looking receptionist offered an early morning smile and asked me to sign a consent form. She passed me to a nurse who ushered me into a small room with a hospital gown. After wrapping myself in the papier-mâché outfit, the nurse told me to get comfortable on the bed. Right!

I wasn't crazy about being sedated while Dr. Stevenson snaked around my colon, but I closed my eyes and waited for the nurse anesthetist to arrive. Unlike the receptionist, the nurse was smiling and upbeat. She found a vein on the first try and placed my arm comfortably on the bed. Like clockwork, the smiling doctor made his entrance. "All set, Eddie?"

I nodded, like I had a choice. The nurse wheeled me into a private colonoscopy room, secured an oxygen mask on me, and attached several devices to monitor my heartbeat, blood pressure, and blood oxygen level. Very reassuring.

"Ready or not, here we go, Eddie," Dr. Stevenson said, of course, smiling. He nodded at the nurse, cueing the IV line. The last thing I remembered was the good doctor whistling a show tune.

FALSE ALARM

Distant voices. I felt dreamy, floating, no desire to move. But soon I cracked my eyelids, and apparently, the devil hadn't invited me into his chamber. Through slits, I watched Kate chat with the nurse. She looked upbeat, though their speech pattern appeared in slow motion. When I blinked a few times, they hovered over my bed like priestesses warding off evil spirits. Kate peered at me and smiled, then giggled at the nurse.

"What's so funny?" I asked, barely audible.

Kate picked up what appeared to be a large glossy negative from the foot of the bed and waved it. "You scared the hell out of me, Eddie," she said, her expression lacking conviction.

My head was still in the clouds. "Then how come you're laughing?"

She giggled again with Nurse Sunshine. "I'm sorry, Eddie, I shouldn't be laughing at your expense. It's just . . ." Giggling again.

I searched her eyes. "Help me here, Kate. I'm in a hospital bed, you waving something at me. Am I dying or what?"

"You didn't prep properly, Mr. Short," the nurse said.

My glazed eyes shifted to the nurse, who shrugged. "I did everything on the list." My body resisted to sitting up.

Kate shoved the negative under my nose and pointed. "Not according to this X-ray. See that shadow? That's your intestine. It's dark and looks very ominous."

I attempted to follow her finger pushing into the intestine. "It does look dark."

"And ominous. Dr. Stevenson had to stop the procedure."

"What?"

"I almost died." She narrowed her eyes. "He rushed into the waiting room and waved this stupid X-ray at me like it was death sentence. I thought you had cancer and almost passed out."

"That's not funny."

"Of course not. But after he told me what happened, I actually thought it was."

Dr. Stevenson entered the room, but this time he wasn't smiling or whistling. "Eddie, I had to stop the procedure."

I nodded, embarrassed. "Kate just told me.

"Didn't you follow the preparation list I gave you?"

My eyes crawled up the ceiling. “I thought so. I drank plenty of liquids, juices, lemonade, water.” I paused, not sure whether to lie. “Except...”

All eyes were on me. “It’s just that the enema was too cold, so I had to wait until . . . ”

“Enema?” Dr. Stevenson’s face matched my foggy head. “Eddie, it didn’t call for an enema.”

“The Fleet enema.” I finally raised my body. “Your instructions called for it to be refrigerated first. I took two of them but only after they warmed up.”

“Enema?” His hand was stuck on his chin. “The instructions called for a Fleet Phospho-soda to be chilled, not an enema.”

“I thought they make enemas.”

“They do, but they make other products. The enema wouldn’t have cleaned you out completely, at least not for a colonoscopy. The Fleet Phospho-soda solution is a saline laxative that pulls water from the body into the bowel. It helps soften the stool and cause a bowel movement.”

“You read it wrong as usual,” Kate said. “Now you have to do the procedure all over again.”

Dr. Stevenson was nodding and finally smiling. “F’raid so, Eddie. But the good news is I’m not charging you for the . . . failed attempt. Set up an appointment with my staff. . . . Oh, and Eddie, this time you won’t have to worry about misreading the preparation process. I have a backup for patients like you. Plenty of purging liquids to clean you out."

"But . . ."

"It's okay," he said, still smiling. "You're not the first to not complete the purging process. Though, I must admit, you're the first with the cold enema story." He chuckled. "I need to make a note of that one."

Kate and her chorus giggled. Again!

As the anesthesia began wearing off, Kate helped me get dressed. "This is why you need to read things carefully, Eddie. See what happens when I'm not around."

I wanted to scold her for shopping for shoes instead of helping me at home, but I kept my mouth shut and let her do all the admonishing.

Kate tied the knot on my sneaker. "This was a complete waste of time. Let's go home."

"What about my chocolate pancakes?"

Franny was still asleep when we returned home around eleven. She had been sleeping more than a newborn, and her appetite had diminished significantly. When she wasn't nibbling on crackers, Franny spent most of the day in her room like a self-imposed prisoner. Kate chalked it up to her new surroundings, but the truth was Franny didn't want to live here. Not that I blame her.

Franny's declining memory was caused, no doubt, by depression, which was exacerbated by her refusal to take antidepressants. Forgetting to put her teeth in for an occasional meal made for comic, yet sad commentary.

Worn out, I trudged upstairs to the bedroom. I shouted down for Kate to remove the extra enema from the refrigerator. I lied to the doctor about taking the second one, which in hindsight, didn't matter.

"You don't want it later?" She laughed.

RESISTING EARLY BIRD

That incomplete colonoscopy wore me out, and I woke up famished. I found Kate reading *Southern Living* on the sofa in the family room.

"Let's go out for a bite," I said.

She eyed the stereo clock. "It's only three o'clock, Eddie. Where do you suggest we go at this hour? Heck, it's not even early bird hour."

Early Bird! Those two words I resisted every time I passed a restaurant with a sign in the window that read, 'Early Bird Special.' Florida was known for its early bird specials; upscale restaurants called them sunset dinners. From 4:30 to 6:00 p.m., retirees flocked to restaurants to find the best deal of the week. Now I didn't mind a bargain, but eating just for the sake of saving money didn't appeal to me. The soup to nuts deal that provided food for the next two days whether it's good or not, was just food!

I recalled that when my mother retired to Tamarac, Florida at sixty-three with my stepfather, she couldn't wait to be part of the landscape, which included "one of those early bird places" her friends told her about. And she wanted Kate and I to participate in her initiation by suggesting we meet at 4:45 p.m. When I pointed out it was a weekday, she said, "It beats not having to eat at an ungodly hour, Eddie."

I couldn't convince my mother that Kate and I usually had dinner after we got home from work.

"Nonsense," Mom had said. "Eat like real people."

I wanted to remind her that "real people" had jobs and kids, so they couldn't eat at 4:45 in the afternoon. Instead, I gently explained that Kate and I probably couldn't abandon our workstations on such short notice.

"Come on, Eddie, I haven't seen you in a while."

There was no winning. "Okay, Mom, where did you have in mind?"

"Your stepfather (she loved calling my stepfather your stepfather) has a coupon for Pasquales, but we have to be seated by five sharp. Otherwise, dessert isn't included."

The D word.

Kate and I worked in Miami then and fought the I-95 rush hour, which basically ran from sunrise to 7:00 p.m. So to appease my mother, Kate lied to her boss about a last-minute doctor's appointment, and I picked her up an hour early. We arrived only one minute after five, but my stepfather, who was standing guard outside the restaurant, charged at us with his bad hip waving a coupon. “Hurry, or we’ll miss the two dollars off per person.”

I wanted to inform him that we already missed it, but he sprinted back to the restaurant.

At the door, I peeled my sweaty shirt off my back. “Can’t we lie to the waitress and tell her there was an accident on I-95?” I asked.

He scowled and said Pasquales didn’t make exceptions. He wasn’t pleased when I insisted on paying for the missed dessert and said under his breath what sounded like “now the meal will feel like it cost more.”

Right, more than the $8.99 deal for a perfect piece of whatever they serve for $8.99, less dessert.

Inside, a sea of cotton ball-headed women blocked my view of my mother. “In the corner,” my stepfather said, pointing. “I told them I needed a table for a special occasion.”

At their age, every day was special. Kate whispered she never would subject our son to this madness.

I kissed my mother on her forehead. “Good to see you, Mom.”

“The waitress kept asking where the rest of our party was,” she said.

Such sweet greetings. “You should have told her we were sitting in traffic.”

"That would only complicate matters, Eddie. I lied and said you were in the parking lot." By complicated, she meant we'd be disqualified for dessert. "You should have taken off earlier, Eddie."

My mother never blamed Kate for anything. "I tried, but my boss wouldn't let me go before the morning break."

"Quick, sit down, the waitress is coming."

My mother smiled at Kate as we settled in. "Hi, darling."

Still worked up from the traffic, we ordered two glasses of chardonnay from the jovial middle-aged waitress with a Southern twang.

My stepfather's jaw dropped. "You can't order wine."

"They just did, darling," the waitress said, smiling.

"But the coupon doesn't include liquor."

The waitress tapped her pencil on the pad and looked at me. "Your call."

I glanced at Kate and begged with my eyes.

"Make that ice tea," she said.

"Me too."

My stepfather beamed. "Same for us."

"That was easy. How about your entrée?"

My stepfather waved the crumbled, limp coupon like it was Flag Day and pointed at the early bird menu. "We'll have this."

The waitress slid her pencil through her hair and held his wrist to read the coupon. "You can't have both, honey."

"What do you mean? The coupon is valid till the end of the month."

The waitress pulled up a chair next to my stepfather. "You're not going to believe this, honey, but if I allow you the early bird and the two-dollar coupon, we'd be paying you to eat. That's not very good for business, is it?" She winked at me.

My stepfather studied the coupon, then the menu. "You sure?"

"Very, honey. Your choice."

My stepfather turned to me. "Eddie, you're the accountant in the family. Which is a better deal?"

I checked the regular menu. "The early bird."

He folded the coupon and handed it to my mother. "Four early birds."

I shook off the early bird fiasco memory and informed Kate that my stomach wouldn't make it to dinner. Not after that—successful colonoscopy. "Quick, where's your mother?"

She nodded at the bedroom. "Been there all day."

"Good, she must be hungry."

Kate closed the magazine and sat up. "I don't get it, Eddie, she's never hungry."

"It's called depression, Kate."

"But she refuses to take anything for it."

We'd been through this before. Given Franny's moments of lucidity, Kate was struggling to accept her mother had given up on life. "You can't force her."

"But she'll die!"

Kate had been agonizing over her mother's deterioration but refused to join a support group for fear of knowing Franny never would be whole again. I sat beside her and wrapped my arm around her shoulder. "There's not much we can do, Kate. Even Jesse couldn't convince her to take the antidepressants. Let's face it, your mother is stubborn. We gotta respect her wishes."

Kate's eyes welled up. "I can't stand to see her this way."

I nodded sympathetically and wiped her tears. "Me neither. Come, let's take her out to eat."

Kate gave me a critical look but surrendered with a nod.

Twenty minutes later we arrived at Captain's on the Bay, a nautical restaurant known for its lobster rolls. It had been in the Hall family name since the fifties. I assumed they were opened all day but when I tried to open the door, it was locked. I peeked through the porthole and saw people scurrying about. I was about to knock when I noticed a sign: Sunset Dinners 5:00-6:00.

I recoiled.

"You should have listened to me, Eddie. I told you they weren't open for lunch."

I checked my watch and swore. "I don't want to wait around for an hour."

"You have another place in mind, Mr. Hungry Man?"

I turned to Franny. "Hungry?"

"Not very, Eddie. We can sit in the car and wait."

No way. A gravel trail led beyond the restaurant to the water. "How about we sit by the bay? They have benches."

With low humidity, it was a perfect afternoon to be outdoors. The bay looked like a mirror. "Pretty, no?" I said, turning to Kate.

She nodded indifferently and sat beside her mother. I strolled to the water's edge and drew in a lungful of air. I appreciated how peaceful the postcard view was and felt lucky to live nearby. I scaled a few rocks into the water and sighed, remembering my father taking me to the beach as a kid–on a sober day. When Jesse was small, we frequented Jones Beach on Long Island where I'd walk him by the hand for a good mile before he got tired. How I yearned for my father to join us, but he was gone by then.

I turned back to the girls and waved. Franny still was in her own world. Despite that, I finally felt at peace for the first time in months. I'm not a fatalist, but the older I got, the more I realized life could change in a flash. Best to live moment to moment. Franny had enjoyed a great life but now believed nothing was left for her.

I filled my lungs again and slowly exhaled. I realized death was inevitable, but everything felt suspended for the moment as I took in the beauty of my surroundings. Life was good. For now.

BUSINESS WITHOUT PLEASURE

Kate decided to whisk her mother to the Bahamas for a few days, hoping the white sandy beach and crystal-clear waters would revive her. Over the years, Kate and I frequented Nassau or Freeport when we were down or just plain exhausted from work. Franny loved to gamble, and Kate was hoping the lights and sounds of the blackjack tables in the casino would encourage her to go on with life.

Quite frankly, we all needed encouragement and a change. Lately, Kate had been sully, sulking, and anxious, which created tension between us. And while I had been there for her, Kate was disconnected from me because she was too connected to her mother's condition.

When I arrived home from dropping the girls off at the airport, a phone message was waiting for me. "Hey, Eddie, what's up?" It was Fink.

I had shared with him—perhaps prematurely—that our new tenant was behind in his rent. Fink knew I wasn't cut out to be a nagging landlord, so he nagged me. As I had mentioned, Fink was successful at whatever he did, but *whatever* was never uttered in our conversations. While I would accept an excuse from the tenant, Fink refused to be taken by anyone, especially some deadbeat guy living in his ninth-floor condo on Biscayne Bay. So his "what's up" translated to, "Did you finally collect the rent?"

Curt Stud had been our tenant for all of two months. Our Realtor highly recommended him after doing her due diligence, meaning she confirmed he had a job, no criminal record, and paid his bills on time. That had sounded okay with me, but Fink wanted more information, so I phoned Stud. His voice resonated as though auditioning for the lead in a Shakespearean play. Perhaps he picked up this elocution from watching first-run movies over the years. Stud was the AMC Theatres manager in Miami and had been in the business back in Zanesville, Ohio, for more than fifteen years. He certainly won an academy award with me by answering all the questions to my satisfaction.

But after only two months, Stud was one month in arrears. I first blamed it on the snail-mail post office, so I waited a few more days. But by the end of the week without a check or a courtesy call, I phoned him. Mind you, I could have been sitting on a golf cart, but business is business. To my dismay, his tenor voice threw out salutations and regrets that he was nowhere near his phone. So like an anxious landlord, I left a friendly, yet terse message: "Please call."

Another two days, still no Curt Stud. I reached for the lease application and called his office.

"AMC Theatres."

Couldn't disguise that voice. "Hello, Mr. Stud. This is Eddie Short, your landlord."

"Oh, hi there." He sounded upbeat and genuinely happy to hear from me, as though I were interested in the movie schedule. "Sorry I couldn't get back to you, but I've been putting in long hours. I'm telling you, you can't get decent help in South Florida. I'm tired of watching the same movies—"

"Mr. Stud, I'm calling about the rent." Familiarity only would complicate matters.

"Oh, I hope you're not going to raise it already," he said with a laugh.

"No, Mr. Stud, but you are over two weeks late, and that calls for a late fee. But if you have a legitimate excuse …"

"What, you haven't received it yet? I sent it well over a week ago. . . . Incompetent post office."

"A week ago?"

"I remember because I was home paying bills at my desk and watching that Robert Redford movie where he was putting the moves on what's her face? The one with the nose."

"Barbra Streisand," I said, helping him along like an idiot.

“Right. He was telling her …”

“Mr. Stud, we have a problem.”

“Darn right we do. I'm calling the post office first thing in the morning. That okay?”

“No, Mr. Stud, that's not okay. You need to put a stop payment on the check and send me a new one.”

A few uncomfortable moments passed. “Mr. Stud?”

“I could do that, except, well, it wasn't a check.”

“You didn't send cash, I hope?”

“God no, I paid with a money order.”

“No problem. Just go to the bank and explain what happened.”

“Bank?”

I felt a headache coming on. “The bank where you purchased the money order.”

“Oh, it wasn't a bank.”

I grabbed a bottle of Advil off my desk and fiddled with the lid while informing him I couldn’t care less where he purchased the money order; he needed to buy a new one.

“No can do. I mean, Eddie, they ain't gonna issue another money order until they investigate the first one. And I can't afford to send another payment. You understand, don't you, Eddie?”

Eddie? And ain't gonna? “Mr. Stud, I'd like you to send me a copy of the money order.”

“You don't believe me, Eddie? I thought we were friends.”

“Excuse me?”

"Friends. You know, landlord and tenant, priest and confessor, husband and—"

"Mr. Stud, I want a copy sent to me immediately!" My voice shifted like a homicide detective.

"You're good. Ever thought of acting? I know an agent—"

"Otherwise, I'll assume you haven't sent it and will be forced to begin eviction proceedings. Get my drift?"

"Who wouldn't? You're not being very reasonable, but since you put it that way, I'll have it in the mail tomorrow."

"Thank you." Exasperated, I hung up and grabbed a glass of water for the Advil.

I returned Fink's call to relate the conversation.

"When did you speak with him?" Fink asked.

"Just a few minutes ago."

"You want me to call him, Eddie? You know, tell him I'm not happy."

I wasn't ready for a showdown. "Let's give him a chance."

"Or, I can make a trip, discuss it in person."

"Fink, it really isn't necessary."

"'Cause, Eddie, I don't like that you're taking the brunt of this."

Fink would do anything for me, but I didn't want him doing time for getting his point across. "I can handle it."

"How's Mom?" he asked, thankfully changing the subject.

"Not too good." When I updated him, he sounded upset. Fink adored my mother-in-law, and she was crazy about him. He began calling her "Mom" after she and his father were an item. His father was widowed—and wealthy after working for his son—and had his eye on Franny for years. When Franny became available, he made his move. She loved being pursued by him—the fast cars, exotic vacations, and the best restaurants in town. And this was only a few years ago. They even considered marriage, but Kate was against it because of his family's reputation. We would have been one happy family if he hadn't died in Franny's bed. Needless to say, that freaked out Kate.

"A shame," Fink said. "She's like a mother to me. If there's anything I can do for you and Kate, let me know."

"I will, and thanks for asking."

"Keep me informed about our tenant, Eddie. Don't be too nice."

"Promise."

Was Fink going to have to pay Curt Stud a visit after all?

HEARTLESS

Weak smiles greeted me at Palm Beach International. In fact, Kate looked worse than her mother.

"You guys gamble all night?" I joked after rolling down the passenger window. Kate didn't answer as she helped her mother into the back seat and buckled her up like a child. When she hopped in the front, I offered her a kiss. She didn't match my intensity and pulled away to buckle up. I tried making small talk, but Franny's eyes were closed, and Kate's woeful expression hinted she was too exhausted. We rode home in silence.

Kate put Franny to bed while I poured two glasses of merlot, then waited for Kate to return from a shower.

I pointed at the wine and was about to toast to nothing in particular when Kate downed hers before I had a chance. She poured another glass.

"Boy, were you thirsty," I said, taking my first sip.

Kate stared at the glass. "I feel so helpless."

I wrapped my arm around her shoulder. "I gather the trip wasn't successful."

Kate shook her head slowly as her eyes welled up. "She's determined to die, Eddie."

I kneaded her shoulders. "I wish I could do something to ease your pain."

She rested her head on my shoulder. "Just hold me, Eddie."

I must have *Sucker* etched on my forehead. Another week and still no rent or word from Curt Stud. I paced, brooding and pondering my next move. After eating a plate of linguine with clam sauce, my stomach was talking. I belched, prompting Kate to turn from some quiz show on TV.

She waved away the toxins. "You're too wound up to be a landlord, Eddie. You should never have let Fink talk you into this. He's up North having a great time, and you're moaning about this rent business all the time."

I stopped in front of the tube. "That was the deal, Kate. I manage the place for a 25 percent interest. A lot of potential is riding on this."

"But it's making you crazy. Look at you, pacing the room like you're about to pounce on somebody."

"Yeah, Curt Stud."

She shook her head. "The way I see it, Eddie, you have two options unless you consider getting Fink involved." She paused to garner my full attention. "But that's not really an option unless you want Stud to disappear."

"I thought of that."

"Well, stop thinking about that one unless you want to join Fink in the big house."

"Bastard."

"You either threaten the tenant with eviction or just wait." Kate shrugged. "Your choice."

I pressed my belly for relief. "Easy for you, Mrs. Trump. You don't have to deal with that deadhead."

She followed my hand circling my stomach. "You want me to call him, don't you? Is that the ploy?"

I waved. "Forget it. That guy will make you dizzy. He always evades the point." My eyes shifted to the tube where a contestant was rattling off the names of the first five Popes like they were her kids.

"He can't be all that bad." She craned her head around me. "I'll call him in about five minutes, right after the show." She looked up at me. "That okay?"

I nodded in desperation. "Sure, why not?"

I left his phone number on her lap and trudged to my cave to distract myself on the computer. But after a half hour, I called out, “Isn't your program over yet?”

When Kate didn’t answer, I opened the door and heard her giggling, adding a few quips, then more giggling. I edged out tentatively to listen.

“Sure, Curt, I understand. . . . No, don't worry, I'll explain it to Eddie. . . . You too. Oh, and thanks for the invitation.” She hung up and turned to find me staring at her. “That was easy.”

I narrowed my gaze. “Exactly what did you mean by ‘I’ll explain it to Eddie?’ And what invitation?”

“Oh, that. Curt said he’d comp us a few movie tickets if we were ever in the neighborhood.”

“Tickets! I don't want no stinking tickets. And the only reason I’d go to his neighborhood is to collect the fucking rent!”

Kate laughed. “Calm down, Eddie. It was nice gesture. By the way, you sound like what's his name in that Mel Brooks movie.”

I threw up my hands. “You’re as crazy as he is. . . . Well, is he sending the rent or not?”

“Rent?”

“Kate!”

“I'm kidding. Don't you have a sense of humor?”

I pointed at her. “Not when it involves your new friend, Curt Stud.”

“Relax, he's sending it.”

"Good. When?"

"When?"

"Yes, when is he sending the money?"

She thought a moment. "He didn't actually say."

I shook my head in disgust. "Christ, Kate, what the hell were you talking about, South Florida weather?"

"Well, that too. And girl stuff."

I was about to explode. "Girl stuff? What, like you're fixing him up with one of your friends?" I raised a finger. "Say, that's not a bad idea. Maybe she can pick up the damn rent."

Kate burst into laughter.

"What did I say?"

"Curt's gay."

I squeezed my eyes. "Gay? How the hell did you find that out?"

"He told me."

I rubbed my eyes and leaned against the wall. "Let me understand this correctly: You asked him about the rent, and he just happened to mention he's gay?"

"Something like that. His roommate has to have open heart surgery and doesn't have health insurance."

"Roommate!" I charged into my cave, rummaged through a Pendaflex file, and yanked out the Key Biscayne apartment file to read the lease agreement. Curt Stud, single. No one else listed. I raced back to Kate and waved the lease, scowling. "He lied to me,

Kate, just like he did about the rent payment. The lease says he lives alone. I'll have that bastard and his broken-heart roommate evicted immediately!"

"Eddie, for goodness sake. What's the big deal? So he has a roommate?"

"Who apparently doesn't have enough money to help him with the rent. . . . That Stud is nothing but a pathological liar."

Now Kate was scowling too. "You've become so callous since you've become a big real estate tycoon. Have a heart."

I sneered. "Not his boyfriend's, that's for sure!"

TO THE POINT!

I should have sought Fink's help sooner. Entering yet another month with no rent in sight, I finally called my business partner to break the news. Obviously, he wasn't pleased and demanded Stud's phone number.

In two days, FedEx delivered the check, which included two months with the late fee and an apology note. The note also mentioned he would be vacating the premises by the end of the month and was forfeiting his security deposit for breaking the lease. Go Fink!

When I contacted my Realtor, Joan, about his departure, she apologized profusely and said she couldn't understand why the screening process had failed. Perhaps Stud's reference from Zanesville had, let's say, a memory gap. She told me she would be happy to look for a new tenant. And why not? She would be entitled to another commission.

My cell phone rang—Joan. Had she found a tenant that quickly? With a smile, I answered it. My expression changed when she informed me Mr. Curt Stud had left the unit slightly, um, untidy. "It's best if you drive down here, Mr. Short, and see for yourself."

Her voice reminded me of Kate's when the shit was about to hit the fan. "Something wrong?"

She rattled off a few innocuous offenses and then something about paint.

"But it was painted just before he moved in," I said.

She waited a few moments as though surveying the condo. "The carpet looks soiled, Eddie. Did Mr. Stud own a dog?"

I closed my eyes. "He wasn't supposed to."

"Well, I think he did unless he suffered from incontinence. In any event, it needs to be cleaned."

Joan greeted me outside the unit with a rather formal smile and handshake. "Please don't be too upset, Mr. Short." But then she opened the door.

I moaned. "Oh, God. What did that bastard do to my apartment?" The place looked as though a tsunami had hit it.

"As I mentioned over the phone—"

"And what's that God-awful smell?" I clamped my nose.

"Urine, I think."

My eyes settled on a large wooden platform supported by the wall. Spotlights dangled from the ceiling, along with different colored beads, squaring it off like some kind of tawdry boudoir. I pointed. "What the hell is that?"

Joan shrugged. "It looks like a stage."

"A stage? What on Earth for?"

"Porno films, I think. You see those brackets coming down from the ceiling? They must have held up a trapeze."

I turned to her. "Porn? Trapeze? What are you saying? They were doing … acrobatics?"

"Looks that way, Eddie."

I scrutinized her. "How do you know this?"

Evidently, she realized her knowledge in such things and blushed. "My son told me."

"Your son?"

"Let me back up a second. My car was in the shop, so my son dropped me off. I asked him to come up for a second. Apparently, he'd seen something similar in one of those … sex movies."

I looked closer, trying to imagine Curt Stud swinging to and fro. *Wait a second . . . Stud?* No wonder his roommate had a bad heart. God knows what else was broken!

"Eddie?"

I turned back to her. "Yes," I whispered.

"How do you suppose you're going to remove that thing?"

"Remove it?"

"From the condo."

Removing it hadn't entered my mind. Killing Curt Stud had. "I don't know. Maybe you can help me?"

Joan stepped back. "Eddie, do you know how much that must weigh?"

I shook my head.

"Anyway, as you can see, that wouldn't even fit through the door."

I scratched my head. "It got in, didn't it?"

Joan motioned me over to the platform. She lifted a skirt at the bottom of the stage. "See, they built it in the apartment."

"Built it?"

"Eddie, you don't think he purchased it from Rooms To Go, do you?"

I shook my head slowly. "No, I don't suppose so."

"You'll have to get a saw, cut it up, and remove it before I can show the unit again." She almost made it sound as though I were the culprit.

I wiped perspiration from my brow. *I needed a fucking saw?*

After cutting up the stage and hauling the pieces downstairs, prompting stares from the neighbors, I made a list of every infraction, the least of which was a urine-stained carpet. After checking the appliances, toilets, and sinks, I discovered Key Biscayne's porno king had the last laugh. Apparently, he had dumped a shovelful of Key Biscayne's finest white sand down the kitchen sink.

I called AMC Theatres but no longer heard Stud's voice with the movie schedule. I cued customer service, and a woman informed me he had left town for personal reasons. I bet! No forwarding address, of course. I hung up and shouted, "Curt Stud, you phony bastard! I bet that's just your stage name."

I waited to calm down before calling Fink. Actually, he took it better than I did. "Not to worry, Eddie, Curt Stud will pay."

DEATH IS FINAL

Denial ain't just a river in Egypt

Mark Twain

Death was inevitable, but some people accelerated it. Take Franny, resolute in her desire to die. She ended up starving herself to the point that Kate and I had to hospitalize her. I never had witnessed a suicide, unless you counted my father's years of heavy drinking, which shut down his heart and liver. But Franny's case was especially painful to accept, given her free and loving spirit. Knowing her, though, I understood. Under similar circumstances, could I work up the courage to reduce my life sentence?

In denial, Kate had invited every professional to our home to persuade her mother to live, including a Santeria healer from Miami. With all the coming and going, the neighbors must have thought we were drug dealers. Our last visitor, a local priest, was also fruitless. "It's in God's hands," he told Kate at the door. Actually, it was in Franny's.

Kate begged me to keep trying, to force some sense into her mother, but I reminded her Franny had a living will, and we were morally, if not legally, bound by her wishes. I did make a final attempt, begging her to hang around and sprinkling in good old-fashioned guilt about how much we needed her. But Franny's fundamental decision rested with her awareness of the crippling dementia—she rationalized at times—and that her dependence on us was totally unacceptable. The woman had class and wanted to leave this Earth with dignity.

"Help me die, Eddie," Franny said on her last day at our house. "You're the only one I can rely on."

I told her I didn't want to do time, attempting a laugh, but she only pleaded more. With no possibility of convincing her, I said I understood and thought she was a brave soul. Weak, she signaled me closer as I got up to leave, her voice a mere whisper. She praised me for being a good husband, friend, and son-in-law. I held her and promised to care for her daughter until it was my turn to leave this Earth.

After entering the hospital, it didn't take long for Franny to start hospice care, where she spent her final days in a private room. Though honestly, in her state of mind, she could have cared less if she had to share the room with Hannibal Lecter. A middle-aged hospice intake coordinator named Carol with dark-rim glasses assured us Mom would have the best of care and conveyed her condolences. She brought us to a room, a respite for family members, where we could spend time between visits with Franny.

We sat there in our own thoughts for the next half hour until Laura showed up, teary-eyed and distraught. Though Kate was still seething over Laura telling their mother about the dementia and had accused Laura of hastening her death, they locked in an embrace, shed tears, and comforted each other. I walked over to the window to give them their space.

When Laura tapped my shoulder, I gave her a brotherly kiss on the forehead and held her tightly. She trembled, but I told her she was safe with me. She believed informing her mother was the right decision and searched my eyes for affirmation, which I couldn't provide.

"Eddie, I don't know what to do."

She was referring to closure, and I advised her to just be herself. "Tell Mom you love her. She may be in a coma, but I'm sure she can hear you."

I guided Laura to Franny's room and closed the door behind her, praying Franny could hear and accept Laura's plea.

Emotional ordeals made me hungry, so I decided to go out to fetch lunch. As I headed to my car, the cell phone interrupted my thoughts. Fink. He asked about Franny, and I estimated the time of her passing. "Within a week, but more likely a few days."

Fink said he was planning to attend the funeral, then mentioned Curt Stud as a pick-me-up. "Stud is back in Zanesville," he said, like he'd accomplished a mission.

"Fink, I don't think I should be a part of this conversation."

He laughed. "You don't want to know that the creep paid for all damages?"

I unlocked the car door and jumped in, fearing some NSA sensor might pick up the airwaves. "That part, yes, just not the gory details."

"Believe it or not, there aren't any."

"Seriously?"

"Define gory."

"End of conversation."

"Just kidding, Eddie. Stud was shocked when my friend showed up at his door." He laughed. "The poor guy pissed himself, swearing it was a mistake. He was willing to write out a check on the spot, only my friend said cash was the only way he'd go away. The bill he handed Stud included a round-trip ticket from JFK and a wild night in downtown Zanesville." Fink laughed again, and I joined in this time.

"Wait, there's more. Stud asked if he could change his pants before going to the bank for the cash."

We shared another laugh. "Thanks, Fink."

"That's what partners are for. Anyway, I don't deposit cash, so I'll bring it with me."

"Great, and thanks for coming. It will mean a lot to Kate." A little white lie.

"And Laura, how's she holding up?"

"It's tougher on her. She and Franny have had a lifetime of differences."

"Tell Laura I look forward to seeing her after all these years." We laughed again. Fink and Laura had a one-night torrid affair soon after her divorce from Billy. I never asked questions.

On the fourth day of Franny's journey, the phone startled us at 6:00 a.m. Kate snapped it up, listened, thanked the caller, and hung up. Her face turned ashen. Franny's breathing had become erratic and labored during the night, prompting the nurse to increase her morphine drip. It was imminent.

"It's not possible," Kate said, crying in my arms. "She can't leave me."

GOODBYE FRANNY

How does one say good-bye to a loved one or a friend? "See you in the next life?" I was brought up to believe in the hereafter, that we would meet our friends and family for one giant cookout. Franny loved cookouts, as did my parents, who I would love to see again—yes, even my father.

I needed to be upbeat and strong for Kate who was struggling with a mix of disbelief, anger, love, and yearning. She'd been distant, down, and contemplative while tackling new projects as though she had a deadline to meet. I had given her space, love, and understanding.

Franny died peacefully with Kate, Laura and me at her bedside. She looked like an angel, my angel. I knew Franny was ready to leave this world but her two daughters weren't ready to let go. This would be perfectly clear for the immediate future.

In fact, lately, I had been a shrink to Laura, who desperately wanted to reconnect with her sister, though Kate wasn't ready. True, they made an attempt soon after Franny's fall, but I believe their mother's passing created a wedge, if only temporary. Laura thanked me for helping her through the hospice period and the funeral, and now, daily baby steps. Laura had reconnected with Fink, probably for nothing more than old times. He was flying out to L.A. for a few days before returning to New York.

I began taking stock of my life, especially at the one-year retirement milestone. Happy Anniversary, Eddie. The year wasn't exactly boring. I made a few friends, attended a few funerals, sunk into depression, got help, made love, became a local hero in the newspapers, encountered old friends, sold a house, bought a new one, and almost took up fly fishing.

I got to thinking when listening to Peggy Lee sing, "Is That All There Is?" What was left for me? I mean, given I survived the first year of retirement, why should I care? Maybe I should be asking what I had missed. Retirees were on the same highway as they were before they retired. Life was not constant even in retirement, so why not consider getting off an exit or two and enjoy the side trips along the way?

A number of my Baby Boomer friends were obsessing that life was closing in, the window of opportunity to accomplish their goals shrinking. If I died tomorrow, how many accomplishments would be etched on my tombstone? Or rather, what would be missing? It was a fair and burning question for those of us Boomers who had buried our passions years ago. Was it too late to recover the passion or explore a new one?

I had an honest and terrific life with Kate, and my relationship with Jesse couldn't have been better. Sure, I'd loved to be a grandparent, but I could handle it if it wasn't in Jesse's cards. So what did I yearn for as my window of opportunity diminished? I wasn't creative and looking to write a best-seller or become a recording artist of the year. Nor had I aspired to be the next Donald Trump or president of my PTA. But snuggling in my cocoon for the rest of my life felt insignificant, as though I was cheating not only myself, but also others of whatever talent I did have. At this stage of my life, could I make a difference in the world?

As the thought of my mortality set in, I'd become more vigilant of my now-what life. I could sit around doing my thing (whatever that was), play a round of golf, smoke a joint in the nude, or read a book on spirituality. But I was beginning to discover there was more to life than just me. I needed to reach out to other people. Don't get me wrong, not having to wake up morning, noon, or night was wonderful, but just too comfortable. I searched my aging brain for answers. Was this it? Work, retire, play, and die?

Those thoughts lingered as I surveyed our home today, watching Kate and our friends during a memorial service honoring Franny. Attending farewells probably was more difficult for our friends in their eighties, such as Morris and his girlfriend, Jenny, who stood out because none of Franny's friends from up North were able to attend. Most people were my age or younger, including Jesse and Rebecca in the corner enjoying their renewed life together. That made me happy, now that I had my cave back.

I was grateful a few close friends from the office joined us on this auspicious occasion. They were chatting with Kate, who hadn't seen them since my retirement luncheon, and were probably wondering about our 24/7 arrangement. Kate occasionally smiled at me and nodded for me to join them. I raised a finger, asking for time. I needed to enjoy our friends and family from a distance. Supposedly, the difference between an Irish wedding and funeral was one less person. Judging from the laughter and positive energy, I believed it. It was so Franny. She loved parties, especially when she was the center of attention. This one was for you, Franny.

I was about to catch up with Kate when Fink approached. "Franny would have loved this."

I nodded. "I know. Thanks for coming."

"Are you kidding? Franny meant the world to me."

I shared Fink's sentiments. My mother-in-law knew how to enjoy life and bring people together.

Fink and I exchanged small talk about the new tenant who was paying his rent on time. But then he eyed Laura, who was searching for someone to rescue her from Billy and probably a discussion about coupons and deals. She caught Fink's stare and smiled, so he excused himself to join them.

I motioned to Kate to a quiet corner. "You holding up okay?" I asked.

She smiled wistfully. "Mom would have loved this, Eddie."

"Yes, she loved people."

"Like you. I guess I never really understood how much you enjoyed people until we moved to Juno Beach. I see the way you interact, like a politician."

"That's doesn't sound like a compliment."

"In your case it is. You should see the smile on your face when you engage in conversation. You are definitely in your element."

I remained silent.

"I wish I had your outgoing personality. I'd probably miss my friends much more. . . . I guess I can be content with my projects."

I tenderly squeezed her chin. "That's sweet. Sometimes I wish I could depend more on myself, get involved in projects, instead of wanting to be entertained by friends."

She touched my hand. "I guess opposites do attract." She winked. "I am attracted to you, Mr. Short."

I kissed her cheek. "And to you, Mrs. Short. I'm extremely into you." I glanced around the room. "It's been a long day."

"Can't wait for it to end." Then she whispered something sexy in my ear. "That's for being there for me."

I smiled. "I know I've been a bit of a burden this year trying to find my way. I apologize."

Kate rubbed my back. "How about we go on a cruise, get out of here for a while? Just the two of us?"

"Sure, where to?"

"You pick. Just make it romantic."

"That would be a cabin with a balcony overlooking Santorini or some other Greek island. Can we afford it?"

Kate smiled. "Sure, now that your insurance guy, Murray, made it right by you."

"Right, Murray. I'm still pissed at him. At least he figured out a way to get me into a safe policy."

"It took a while, but he came through. I still can't believe you threatened to stand in front of his office with a sign, Is Murray Watching Your Money?"

"I would have Kate, I swear."

Kate touched my arm. "At least that chapter is behind us." Kate nosed over at Billy now chatting with Morris. Poor Morris was checking his watch. "I'm sure Billy can find us a deal on a cruise."

"That's for sure." I smiled.

"Then maybe when we return, we can think about moving."

I jerked my head. "What, where to?"

"You're too lonely up here."

"I made a few friends."

"Yeah, but your close friends are south, in Broward County. That's where we should be."

"I don't understand. When did you get this idea?"

Kate shrugged. "Been reading. You'd be surprised how many retirees leave their homes for a different environment, only to return after boredom paralyzes them. It might be nice to spend a few months enjoying the mountains, but it must get lonely without friends or even neighbors."

"We don't live in the mountains. We're only an hour away from civilization."

Kate laughed. "A long hour. I know you miss your friends," she said, nodding at a few across the room. "They miss you too. They told me."

"Really?"

"On Franny's grave."

"Whoa, Franny isn't in a grave. She's scattered over the ocean."

"That's her grave, Eddie."

I remained pensive. "I've been thinking about my own life lately, Kate, and there's something we should discuss."

She lifted a brow. "Oh?"

"*Our* lives, actually, because mine affects yours."

"What's going on in that head of yours, Mr. Short?"

"Later, when we're alone."

"You can't do this to me. I'm a woman. I need to know now. What, you're leaving me?"

I burst out loud. The room froze with everyone looking at us. "Joke," I announced.

"I hate when you do this."

I smiled. "I know."

EPILOGUE
Reinventing Eddie

The bedroom always has been our haven. Besides making love, Kate and I read, think, talk, and play, the latter of which leads to the first activity. Right now, Kate is reading a book, probably another romance novel, while I stare at the ceiling in thought.

I peer over at Kate. “Ready for my big plan?”

“Uh huh.”

“You’re obviously tired because you haven’t asked once since the crowd left. I decided to do something productive with my life.”

“OK, Eddie. Do I need to get a pad and pencil?”

I’m serious, Kate.” I prop up on my elbow.

Kate doesn’t stop reading. “Sounds good, Eddie.”

I know she’s not listening, so I ask if she wants to make out.

“Sure.”

I slip my hand under the sheets and inch up Kate’s thigh.

She closes her book to block my hand. “Eddie, can’t you see I’m reading? Besides, we just did it a few hours ago.”

Obviously, she’s forgotten we used to make love more than once a night. That was a lifetime ago before Viagra. I slide out my hand. “I read somewhere that 80 percent of Boomers plan to work into their seventies.”

Work is a word that no longer applies to my wife. “Good for them, Eddie.” Then she smiles. “Oh, I get it, you decided to do tax returns.”

“Hold on.” I sit up. “That’s not what I had in mind.”

Kate sets her book on the night table and turns to me. “So what, you’re going back to school to learn a trade? Quite honestly, Eddie, I don’t think you can handle school.”

I smile to humor her. “I always thought I could be a rocket scientist if I put my mind to it.”

She gives me a look. “That’s for left-brain people. You’re more … in between.”

“What’s that supposed to mean?”

Kate shrugs. “You told me you failed algebra twice and never made it through chemistry. And that was in high school.”

I raise my hand. “Once. I failed algebra once.”

“Whatever.”

“We’re getting off course as usual. I said productive, as in volunteer.”

“Oh, then why didn’t you say so?”

Women never let you finish. "I was thinking more like Jimmy Carter's organization."

Kate ponders it, then smiles. "Habitat for Humanity. You're kidding, right? I mean, you can't tell the difference between a hammer and a nail. What would you do, be the errand and sandwich boy?"

"Funny." I scowl. "You're not very encouraging, Kate."

She nods. "Sorry, Eddie, I couldn't resist. I'm sure the organization can find a place for a constructionally challenged person."

Why did I bother bringing this up? "Just because I can't swing a hammer doesn't mean I can't help. I can screw better than you can."

"Touché. But not right now."

I lean in. "I've had a good life; we both have. But we only volunteer once a year at the food shelter for Thanksgiving. I was thinking something longer term." I search her eyes.

Kate meets mine. "Seriously? You'd rather hit a few nails than do tax returns?"

"Are you kidding? Anything but tax returns! Besides, construction is right up your alley, partner." I nudge her in the side.

Kate nods, knowing where this is going. "True, and we can meet new people."

"Exactly, with similar interests."

"Since when are you interested in carpenters?"

"You know I like all kinds of people. Besides, there must be at least one other accountant with Carter's group." I smile. "This way we won't miss our friends as much. The truth is, Kate, I'm beginning to really like living here."

"Are you of sound mind?"

"Yup. I made an executive decision: Jimmy Carter and the Shorts. What do you think?"

Kate nods. "Well, yeah, we can give it a shot if that's what you want."

"I do. And I can thank my shrink for helping me get through my … transition period. I'm learning to take one day at a time and figure out where I'm going over the next thirty years." I smile. "OK, maybe twenty. But the point is there are so many things I can and will do. Habitat for Humanity is a start. That's the plan. I probably should have begun the process before I retired." I pause. "It beats hanging around here all day. Plus, the work is interesting. I've done research. Who knows, maybe next year we can help preserve the rainforest in South America or read to the blind here?"

"Eddie, I thought you were off your pills."

"Life is my new serotonin, Kate. This will add meaning to it. Yours too. Look, it's a small way of giving back. I guess hitting sixty, being retired and relatively healthy made me wonder how long I have and what I can do now. I'm looking to reinvent myself."

Kate laughs. "You sound like you finally thought this through, Eddie. Not like when you first retired."

"I have. And Jesse thinks it's a great idea."

Kate frowns. "You talked to Jesse before me?"

"Don't you?"

"Yes, but ..."

"He promised to water your plants once a week."

"He said that?"

"Actually, Rebecca did, but he agreed."

"You can always count on women."

"I certainly have." I squeeze her and plant my lips on her delicate, unpainted mouth. "Wanna make out?"

ABOUT THE AUTHOR

Fred Lichtenberg is a native New Yorker who lives with his wife in Jupiter, Florida. He has one son. Formerly with the IRS, Fred's passion for writing drove him to change hats and become a full-time writer. In 2013, Fred published his third novel, *Deadly Heat at The Cottages: Sex, Murder, and Mayhem*, a mix of zany characters and crazy situations in a fun place called The Cottages. Fred is also the author of two previous works: *Hunter's World*, a murder mystery set on New York's Long Island, which was released by Five Star Publishing in May 2011; and his second murder mystery, *Double Trouble,* that is set in South Florida, New York, Las Vegas and Cancun, Mexico (2012).

In addition to writing mystery novels, Fred has written shorts stories and a one-act play *titled The Second Time Around ... Again*, about finding love in a nursing home, at the Lake Worth Playhouse.

Fred is an active member of the Mystery Writers of America and International Thriller Writers.

CONTACT

Website: fredlichtenberg.com

Facebook: http://on.fb.me/1s1hcRm

Amazon

If you have enjoyed this book by Fred Lichtenberg, please consider leaving a review.

OTHER PUBLICATIONS BY THIS AUTHOR

Deadly Heat at The Cottages: Sex, Murder, and Mayhem

Hunter's World

666 Kendall Drive

Double Trouble

Paradox Promotions
Covers & Formatting
http://bit.ly/paradoxcovers

31117029R00162

Made in the USA
Middletown, DE
18 April 2016